PROBLEM SOLVED

PROBLEM SOLVED

STEPHANIE PERRY MOORE

KENSINGTON PUBLISHING CORP.

DAFINA BOOKS are published by

Kensington Publishing Corp.
850 Third Avenue
New York, NY 10022

ISBN: 978-0-7394-8936-9

For Chan and Laurie Gailey
(A great football coaching couple)

Thank you for your years of service in helping people.
You both have blessed my family, and I'm forever grateful!
I hope every young person follows your model
and puts God first in all things.
Only then will they have their problems solved.

Acknowledgments

Everyone who knows me or my writing understands that I love football. I believe if I were a male I would have played. As a spectator I learned that playing isn't easy. Like life you win some, lose some, some get rained out, and some end in a draw. I've learned that playing is about being able to midstream adjust when problems arise. The ones who stay upbeat and take their woes to God are the ones who win in life.

So if I was to play my favorite game, I'd be the quarterback. You know, the one whose job it is to lead his team to victory. Being young people, I strongly believe you are all leaders. Don't look for the worst in situations, bring out the best in yourself by doing things God's way. Just remember that a great leader is only as good as his followers. Come to think about it, on my writing team I am the QB. Here is a thank you for the best squad ever.

To my family, parents Dr. Franklin and Shirley Perry, Sr., brother, Dennis and sister-in-law, Leslie, my mother-in-law, Ms. Ann and extended family, Bobby and Sarah Lundy, I can always count of you. My problems are minimal because I have you to lean on. Like ferocious offensive linemen, thanks for blocking my drama.

To my publisher, Kensington/Dafina Books, and especially my editor, Selena James, I am grateful you're there to help me through this process. My errors get solved when you get into the writing mix. Like the accurate kicker, you help me score the needed points to make this series a winner.

For my writing team, Calvin Johnson, James Johnson, Ciara Roundtree, Jessica Phillips, Randy Roberts, Ron Whitehurst, Vanessa Davis Griggs, Larry Spurill, John Rainey and Teri Anton, I'm a stronger writer because of your input. The honest advice you gave created the best product in the end. Like tenacious defensive linemen, you sacked and attacked the issues and made sure no negative writing yards were gained.

To the special young men in my life, Leon Thomas (foster son), Franklin Perry III (nephew), Kadarius Moore (nephew), Dakari Jones (Godson), Dorian Lee (Godson), and Danton Lynn (Godson), I know you'll do great things. May this novel help you see that though life won't be fair, God will see you through. Like a dominate tight end, I pray you'll block out life's drama, and catch the most unattainable dreams.

To my girlfriends' sons, Devan Dixon, Colby Clark, Breshad Perriman, Antonio Jr. & Austin London, Bryant Bolds II, Roy Palmer Jr., Brandon & Brian Bradley, Justin & Jordan Peace, and Chandler, Canyon, & Cole Smith, your accomplishments make me proud. I hope this novel helps you know God created you to be strong in Him. Like a fierce linebacker, I know you'll stop trouble in its path and cause fumbles to work in your favor.

To my spunky chicks, Sydni and Sheldyn, I love you dearly. Though I have personal drama, I work through it to show you we can't ever stop reaching for our dreams. Like awesome wide receivers, you, my next generation, catch my enthusiasm and soar higher towards many touchdowns in this life.

To my husband, Derrick Moore, I am sane because of your support. Thanks for trying to give me the desires on my heart and solve my problems. You're still my most favorite running back, leading our home towards God.

To my readers, I'm motivated to write because I care about your life. Remember to take your worries to Christ. Like the most crafty defensive backs, always move to stay on the ball and take it out of the enemy's hand.

And to my God, I am thankful you allowed me to make a difference through writing. And thanks for taking the wheel in my life. You're my life's coach. No play happens without your call.

Contents

1. Understanding the Difference   1

2. Speaking It Plain   17

3. Walking with Pride   33

4. Seeing No Color   49

5. Intersecting with Trouble   63

6. Revealing True Facts   77

7. Mixing It Up   93

8. Convicting the Heart   105

9. Restoring What Matters   119

10. Glorifying God Always   135

11. Being a Gentleman   149

12. Pampering Only Gold   165

13. Speaking Problems Away   181

14. Getting Great Encouragement   197

15. Doing Life Right   213

~ 1 ~

Understanding the Difference

Now, I know better. When a white person looks at me, they either see a rising football star or just another hoodlum. I didn't get the latter look often because I was known for my moves on the field. I guess I was sheltered. I didn't have much interaction with people of a different culture or race. So when Saxon and I stood at the steel hotel doorway of our introduction to society Beautillion party that was getting a bit out of control, and the manager stood in front of both of us looking like he wanted to grab us by the necks and throw us in jail, I didn't know how to take it. Racism was hitting me straight in the face. No part of me liked that.

But Saxon seemed familiar with the disturbing actions of the man. He took the lead and said, "Alright, man, we hear you. We're just having a little fun. Dang. We pay our money just like everybody else. You just trying to get on us 'cause we're black."

"Now, son, there's no need to toss the race card around," the red-faced manager said, looking away.

"Wait, hold up," Saxon said as he stepped up into the man's beaming red face. "I am not your son."

"Okay, you need to step back then," the manager asked, realizing he wasn't dealing with a punk.

Saxon and I had never been cool. Truthfully, we both had egos. We were both *the man* at our respective schools. It was going to be interesting playing ball with him at Georgia Tech in the next couple of months. He was a wild guy and I didn't have much respect for the dude. However, my life hadn't been perfect either. So in some ways we were cut from the same piece of sirloin. And I felt a bond with him when the manager tried him.

Though there wasn't alcohol in the room where the party was jumping off, I wasn't a fool. I could smell Saxon had been tipping in someone's jar. The last thing he needed was to be hauled off for letting his mouth get the best of him. So I pushed him back into the room with the rest of the folks.

I said to the riled-up guy, "I got this boy. Get in there."

Over my shoulder Saxon said, "Tell me something then. Because you'd better talk some sense into him. Shoot, I'm about to bust a—"

"Man, go," I said, grabbing the doorknob and trying to shut Saxon inside. "Sir, I'm sorry for my friend."

"You don't need to apologize for me," Saxon said as the door closed.

I looked over at the manager and said, "Really, sir, we'll keep it down."

The manager nodded in approval of my words. "I'm just saying, young man, this is a respectable hotel. We didn't mind having your event in the ballroom, but we don't allow room parties, and if you can assure me that you people will keep it down, then I won't bother you."

Again this man was ticking me off. *You people*. What in the heck did he mean by that? I guess he saw fire in my eyes. He backed away.

"Well, I'll leave you to your guest now," the manager said.

I closed the door in anger. Saxon came up to me. His breath was stronger than before.

"Want a little," he said, holding out a bottle of gin.

"Naw, man, I'm straight," I said to him as I looked around the place for his gorgeous sister.

Saxon followed me. "See, wh . . . white men think they can talk to the black man any kinda way. My dad gets that crap all the time on his job, but I won't ever let someone think they can handle me without dis . . . spect."

"You mean respect, Sax," I said, trying to keep up with what he was saying.

"Whatever, man, you know what I'm saying. You feel me, too. I saw the heated look on your face when you came back in here. He said something that ticked you off, right?"

I didn't respond. Saxon grabbed my shirt. He shook me.

"Let's go jack him up. We need to teach him a lesson," the drunk boy said.

Taking his paws off me, I said, "Boy, go party. We both need to cool down."

Then I stopped his sister. I couldn't go get with her, though, because she was dancing with some other dude. But as I watched him rub his hands up her fine thighs, I knew I had to let her know how I felt.

However, someone was banging on the door from the outside. My first thought was that the manager had come back too soon. And if it was him, maybe Saxon's idea wasn't such a crazy one after all.

Opening the wooden door, frustrated, I said, "What?"

"Boy, you can't yell at that pretty lady," Saxon said over my shoulder at the sight of my sister. "Come in, come in."

"Sax, get back," I said as he tried to grab her butt. "Your cousin will get you, man, and my dad will, too."

"Oh, Payton, dang, that's Tad's girl? Payton, you look different," Saxon said. "I didn't mean no harm."

"We're cool, Sax," Payton said to him.

"What's up?" I asked her.

She said, "Mom and Dad are in their room on the floor below and want to see you. Folks have been complaining about the noise, Perry."

If I wasn't mad enough already, I was really boiling then. We were just teens having fun. Shucks, the music wasn't that loud.

"You staying or what?" I asked my sister.

"Naw, Tad is coming after he gets off and I gave him Mom's room number."

Shutting the door as we entered the hall, I said sarcastically, "That was smart."

She hit me. Though Payton was kidding, I clammed up. We walked to the elevator in silence.

"What's up with you? I was just joking," she asked as she pushed the button for our parents' floor once we got on.

"Not you, sis," I said as we got off the elevator. "I'm just tired that's all. And I don't want Dad going off on me tonight. I'm not in the mood."

My dad opened the door as if he was waiting for me to arrive. "Junior, I can hear you guys."

I heard noise as well, but the bass beat sounded off. I figured I didn't need to argue with him. I'd let him speak his peace and then I'd be on my way.

"Look, you asked for your own room and I agreed to pay for it. Don't make me regret that decision. The hotel manager called me and said he's been getting complaints about the noise. I knew you were going to have some of your friends over, but boy, don't y'all tear up nothing. And kids can't be drinking in there. Be responsible."

"Dad, I got it," I let out before turning to head back.

"Junior, I'm not finished talking to you."

Sighing and facing him again, I said, "What else, Dad?"

"Look, son, I'm not trying to spoil the party. If that was the case, I would have come down there myself. Just know the rules are different for black kids. Some white folks only tolerate so much. So don't give them a reason to shut your fun down, understand?" he asked.

"Got it."

He said, "Now, Payton, go with him and make sure things stay in line."

"But Dad, Tad's coming here," my sister said.

"Good, he and I need to have a little chat and then I'll send him your way. I don't want y'all too close." He shut the door on both of us.

My sister vented. "Ugh!"

She took the word right out my mouth. We looked at the elevator and saw a lot of people were waiting for it. Payton suggested we take the stairs up one flight. I agreed. When we got around the corner, awfully loud rock music was coming from a room. I peered inside and saw tons of white kids jamming. Then it hit me. What my father was hearing was from around the corner, not from above.

This blond-headed dude came out into the hall. "Hey, y'all are welcome to come in."

Naw, man, we're straight," I said to him, "But tell me something, are you getting any complaints on the noise from the hotel?"

"Complaints, naw, dude." He looked at my sister and smiled like he wanted her.

"That's my sister, but she's taken," I leaned in and said to him before quickly realizing he was just as drunk as Saxon.

"Cool, man, y'all come back," he said.

Payton and I both laughed and we headed to our jam. When we arrived, the hotel manager was walking back toward our door. I wanted him to ask me to keep things quiet.

"Mr. Skky, the noise seems to be growing from this room. I'm afraid I need you to ask your guests to leave. You understand?"

I laughed. "Sir, we just left the party down below us and they have their speakers blasting louder than ours. And since you're not asking them to curtail their fun, maybe you'd better look the other way on our fun as well. Not unless you want me to report this to your superiors? Are you understanding me?"

"Oh well, Mr. Skky, no need to get upset. Just keep the noise down as best you can. Sorry I bothered you." The manager turned and walked away.

I was glad I had caught him being unfair. However, I was saddened to know things like that happen to black kids. But at least it felt good fighting injustice the right way and winning.

Getting back on the floor where the party was, Payton was excited to see her boyfriend standing out front of the door.

"Hey, baby!" she ran up to him and said.

I didn't have any problems with it. Though I was her little brother, I was very protective of my sister. However, I liked Tad, too. He was a good guy. I actually sort of admired a lot of his ways. He was a strong believer in God and I know I wasn't there yet, but I was certainly striving to hopefully have that kind of relationship with God myself.

"Where y'all been? Your father told me you were up here. I have been waiting up here for a bit," he said to the both of us after they let go of their embrace.

"Nothing, my brother just stopped off at another party."

"Dang, y'all been party-hopping without me? Nobody coming on to my girl, are they?"

I looked at Payton and she at me. I knew she didn't want me to say anything. She was hot and Tad knew it.

"Oh, so somebody was!" he exclaimed, and I could see that he valued my sister.

She opened the door, ignoring him, and walked inside. The place was more packed than we had left it, and some of the people I saw in the small cramped room weren't even at the ball, but when there was a party, I shouldn't have been surprised that it could draw folks from everywhere.

I frantically scanned the room looking for Savoy, but I couldn't find her. I hoped that she hadn't left. Even though I had apologized for messing up our relationship, somehow I felt I still needed to explain that I cared.

"Oh, so what's up? You looking for my cousin, huh?" Tad said to me.

Tad and I were cool. I think he liked me a little bit better than he liked his first cousin Saxon, Savoy's brother. And that is probably because I had some type of morals. I wasn't all the way on the Holy Holy side of the scale, but I certainly wasn't slumming in the gutters with Satan like Saxon either. But I had done his cousin wrong and I didn't know how he'd feel about that. Shucks, I didn't even know if he knew what had gone down between the two of us.

"Oh, so what, you can't talk to me? I know you looking for Savoy. And I know what went down between the two of y'all," he said.

Though I knew he could be understanding, I mean Tad was even practicing abstinence—my sister was having a hard time keeping her loins under control. If it wasn't for Tad leading the Lord's way, they would have fallen a long time ago.

"Man, look, I'm not perfect so don't think that I am," Tad surprised me by saying. "I want to get with your sister so bad, but you know I just ask the Lord to keep me wanting to please him more than I want to please my own flesh and so far that has helped. Everybody makes mistakes; my cousin isn't perfect either. You guys are about to go to college so there is no reason why . . . If you want to talk to her, be real with her. Y'all can work something out."

"You think she'll listen?" I finally opened up to him and asked.

"I don't know, there she is over there," he said, pointing to the girl I couldn't find. "Why don't you go ask her?"

I nodded and headed over in her direction.

She wasn't smiling and she wasn't walking toward me. Thankfully she wasn't walking away.

"Hey!" I said nonchalantly when I got right upon her face. She replied, "Hey."

"Wanna dance?"

"I've been dancing all night, I'm a little tired of dancing," she said.

"You want to step outside in the hall and talk? We can walk around the hotel."

"Yeah, we can do that," she said.

I was so excited to have a bit of her time. I mean, I didn't deserve it. We said we were going to be in a committed relationship and I broke that vow not even more than a month after we made it. How could she ever trust me again? But when I looked into her gorgeous dark brown eyes, I knew I had to try. It messed with me a bit to see her in someone else's arms. And although it was all my fault, if there was anything I could do to reverse it, I had to try.

"So what did you want to talk about?" she asked when we got outside by the pool.

Being a popular guy, I could tell when girls wanted to get with me. They would wink, laugh at nothing, or stand real close to me; wear revealing clothes and sometimes even give me their underwear. But Savoy's distant stance was far from inviting. Again she asked with her arms folded, "What did you want to talk about?"

I didn't know how to begin so I looked away. Then she replied, "You know what? Maybe this wasn't a good idea, the two of us being alone up under the moon, stars, and all. I can't do this, Perry."

Before she walked away, I grabbed her hand. "I messed up. I told you I messed up. Wait, Savoy, don't leave!"

"Why should I stay?" she asked.

"Because you have to know how I feel."

She chuckled. "Come on, Perry, your actions told me how you feel about me. I'm not angry with you, I told you that, but you can't expect me to forget that it happened."

"No, no. I know you can't forget, but I don't want you to dwell on it."

"Yeah, right!" she said, stepping away from me. "There are some nights I can't even sleep because all I can do is imagine you in Tori's arms."

"Okay, maybe we can't be boyfriend-girlfriend anymore, maybe that was too strong of a title for us anyway, but can't we just hang out—do this thing, see where it takes us?"

"Why should I reinvest time in something that I tried and didn't work out?"

As she was talking, I didn't hear what she was saying. All I could see was her juicy lips asking me to kiss them. So I did. At first she was resistant, pushing me back a little, but her lips never left mine. And then she melted some, didn't give me so much turmoil, and then I knew what I felt for her she felt for me as well. We weren't headed to the altar or anything, but in that kiss, in that moment, in that embrace, I knew we weren't through. And when we pulled away, Savoy knew it, too.

"I guess us spending time together in the end isn't going to hurt anybody, but I am ready to go back to the party now. Perry, I mean—we can't do this! Kissing me and all, why are you trying to confuse me? You cheated on me, okay?"

"I was wrong and stupid, I'm sorry! Can't you see I feel something for you?"

"Yeah, and that's what worries me, because maybe what you're feeling is something that could get us both into trouble, and we'll both end up regretting our actions like you say you are regretting yours and Tori's. I don't know, maybe it's not a good idea for the both of us to hang out. I gotta go back now."

She didn't even wait for me to catch up to her as she opened the back door of the hotel and walked through the ballroom corridor. I wanted to reach out and pull her close to me, but I had to realize that it just wasn't the place where the two of us were anymore and it was my fault. When the elevator door opened, she had her hand on her hip and her mouth looked pissed.

I got in, then she said, "You know what? I'm just going to take the stairs. I'll see you up there."

"I can walk with you," I said.

"Nah."

She let the elevator doors shut with me inside. Alone. Or I thought I was alone. The white dude from the party earlier was behind me, squatting in the corner on the floor.

"Dang, man, that must be your girl. She looks mad, dude. What did you do?"

Even though the beer had him talking sluggishly, his relationship senses were keenly awake.

"Man, you black boys are dumb. There's no way I'd let a girl with a butt looking that good get away from me." He went to press the elevator buttons. "Open up the door. I want to go talk to her."

"Awh naw, partna, mmm-mmm, you stay back," I said as I grabbed his arm and took it away from the buttons.

"That's where I know you . . . you're that state football dude that plays all good and going to Tech and all. I'm a Bull-dog, man!"

"I hear yah, partna."

"Well, let me just say this: I always heard that black boys

have a lot of pride. And that might be fine, but that's why you're in this here elevator with me instead of with that girl."

When the elevator opened again, it was his floor. He said, "You better lay down your pride and think about what I'm saying and go after what you want, you understand?"

I never caught his name. He was cool and he was drunk, but he had a point. Savoy wasn't going to make it easy for me to get back in her good graces, and maybe that made me like her more.

The next day we were in church and I couldn't figure out why my dad looked so uncomfortable sitting a couple of seats down from me. After all, the preacher was giving the word. I remember being a little boy and my dad saying to me, "You might be upset, son, that you don't have that train you want, but you can't come to the Lord's house pouting. God can't work on your heart if you're not open to hear Him." And ever since then, even when I've been upset, I always made sure I checked my attitude at the door. After all, I clearly understood having a hard heart only made it difficult for the Lord to fix me.

My sister and my dad were close, so since she sat right beside me, I leaned over and said, "What's up with Dad?"

She looked down at our father and replied, "What are you talking about? He's listening. Shhh, I'm listening, too!"

My mom, who was sitting right beside my father, had a big smile on her face. I couldn't believe the two women who cared for him so much couldn't see he was stressed to the max. I don't know why my dad and I weren't real partners and I don't even know if I wanted us to be, but I knew the females in his life were missing that something serious was going on. And I did love my pops so maybe it was my job to get to the bottom of his troubles.

My pastor said, "If you turn your Bibles to the Old Testament and look into the book of Joshua, tenth chapter, I want to take my text from the twelfth verse."

When I thought about getting closer to the Lord, I knew one way to do that was by reading His word more. And sometimes the Old Testament was a little hard for me to understand, so I was really looking forward to the fact that our pastor was going to dissect that text. I read the words out loud with the rest of the congregation but I didn't really understand them—Joshua was trying to fight some kings, and I couldn't make out the rest so I listened on.

"Church, you must understand," our pastor said, "this was a day none had seen before and none after it had ever occurred. A lot of us out there have problems and troubles and this text should help you understand that the Lord will answer when you speak to your problem. You see, in order for Joshua to have an advantage to defeat the kings and save Israel, he couldn't fight at night, so he told the sun to stay up and told the moon not to come. He believed wholeheartedly in his request, and with the conviction of faith that he possessed, the Lord answered."

I went back through and read the text, and I could understand all that the pastor was describing, how awesome it was to understand the Lord's word. Speaking to your trouble and believing that the Lord would work it out was definitely a principle I wanted to take in.

Our pastor closed by saying, "So if you have a downpour of trouble in your life, you must say, 'Rain, rain go away!' If things seem too dark, you must say, 'Sun, shine!' If you want to know what your future holds, talk to the stars to shine brighter so you can follow them. In essence, people, I am saying, take it all to God, talk to your troubles, and the Lord will hear. Believe—He will answer and you will be free!"

I stood up at the end of the message, for the first time in

my life clapping. I didn't know what I was going to face. Graduating high school and going on to college, I was expected to perform athletically, but I knew in this message that God was showing me another way to be victorious. I could now claim Joshua 10:12 and speak my troubles away.

When we got home, my dad was quiet at dinner, too. Again I was really trying to figure the dude out. Payton would ask him a question and he'd mumble some answer off. My mom asked him to pass the mashed potatoes and he handed her over the green beans.

Clearly he was preoccupied with something heavy. "Pops, you okay?" I said across the table.

"Oh yeah, son. Ummm. J-just. Yeah, I'm fine. I gotta go into work, though."

"You gotta go into work?" my sister said.

"I know you just got in from college, baby, but we have the whole summer."

"No, we won't, Dad. Remember, I'm taking classes."

See, that was really weird. He always knew what was going on in my sister's life. He forgot that she was only going to be home for a couple of days before going back to summer school. Yeah, the man was really off. He didn't even finish all of his dinner before he got up to head over to work. He said a few things to my mom, kissed her on the cheek, and was out. Then it dawned on me—Jayboe told me my dad was having money issues. The dealership wasn't as profitable as I wanted to believe. Not that I thought a drug dealer knew everything, but maybe there was something to Jayboe's claim. About thirty minutes after my pops left, I made some excuse to get out into the streets myself.

My moms was cool with it and just told me to be in before dark. I felt kind of weird following my dad, but what if I went to the dealership and his ride wasn't there? I had caught him cheating once—was he back to his old ways? Thankfully I was relieved to see the demo car he was driving at the front of the building. Through the glass I could see him on the phone, irate. Though I could not make out who he was talking to, it was very clear that it was not a happy conversation. He even kicked the back of a chair in. At that moment I banged on the glass.

He motioned for me to go over to the side door and he unlocked it. "You have got to be kidding me, Stan," he said as he held up one finger for me to give him a second. It wasn't fair what God was doing to us. I just couldn't tolerate it.

"You can't tell me to calm down. You know what? My son just arrived. I need to call you back."

"What's up, partna, you need some cash?" he said to me, changing his tone as if the world were sunny.

"Naw, Dad, I'm straight. I just wanted to come and talk to you if that's all right?"

"You wanted to talk to me? What's going on, you got girl troubles?"

"Naw, Dad, I'm worried about you."

"Worried about me?" he said again, acting like that was insane. "Son, I'm fine!"

"Come on, Dad. Why don't you level with me? I have been seeing you scratching your head lately, frowning. I just saw you kick the chair. What's going on? Word's out on the street that you haven't been selling as many cars as usual. Everything okay?"

"Son, you have to go to school. You don't need to be worried about my troubles."

"So you're admitting that you have them?"

"No, that's not what I said. I'm just saying I need you to worry about you. I got me, I'm fine."

"Dad, you always talk about me growing up and being a man. I mean, your problems are my problems. What's going on? Can't you be straight with me?"

"Cool, you want to know—have a seat," he said as we sat at one of the sales desks.

"It's hard being a black dealer with the corporate, son."

"What do you mean?" I asked, really wanting to have a deep conversation with him.

"Although we do pretty well and we've been here for years—your grandfather started this dealership."

"Yeah, I remember," I said.

"Most of the other dealerships are third and fourth generation, not two, like the one I inherited from my dad. And if your automotive franchise doesn't have lots of cash in the bank, when tough times hit," he said, "well, it's even harder for a newer business to survive."

Dad didn't have the biggest building, but he owned it. The problem came when he added another line of luxury cars to the business. Having to have higher priced cars on the lot was making the business less successful. Looks like he bit off more then he could chew. My dad continued, "I should have kept it like my dad had it. However, I bought into wanting to sell these top-of-the-line cars. What I didn't realize is that the only times those deals are made available to black people is when a white dealer has already been unsuccessful. I'm finding out stuff that is quite frankly really disturbing me. Son, I have tried to make you think that the world is equal; black or white—it doesn't matter. As long as you have the skills and the money, you can be a player, but that is simply not true. Sometimes corporate America does things to keep black businesses down."

"You're saying they sold you a business that they knew couldn't do well?"

"Yeah," he strongly replied, making sure I was understanding the difference.

~ 2 ~

Speaking It Plain

"Y'all know I ain't about to graduate, right?" Damarius said to Cole and myself.

Both of us stopped and looked at our boy. We were eight days away from getting our diploma; we had been friends for years, had each other's backs—been in and out of trouble, teammates. I mean, in some aspects we were one! And if he weren't graduating, it would hurt me more deeply than he'd ever know.

"What you talking 'bout, man?" I said, hoping he was just joking.

"You serious about this, huh?" Cole said as he came up from the bench press where Damarius was spotting him. "Man, what's the problem? I saw your last report card," Cole said to him. "You passed everything. What do you mean, you're not graduating?"

"The stupid graduation test," Damarius said as he walked toward the corner, not able to look either one of us in the eye.

The state of Georgia had benchmark tests you had to pass along the way which were now in effect. We didn't have to take them in the third or fifth grade, but in the eighth grade and now for us seniors, they were mandatory. If you didn't pass the test, you were not able to move on to the next grade, or in our case, graduate. It was holding back a lot of students across the state, but thankfully there were options in place for those who didn't pass. And it was making kids all around understand the course material so they wouldn't be held back. Damarius kicked his water bottle across the room.

"Man, I just didn't want to tell y'all. I just didn't want to deal with it!" he said, real emotional.

"Man, I got my scores back and barely passed the thing," Cole replied.

I had exceeded in every area—for me it wasn't that hard—but it wasn't about me right now and I didn't want to make either of them feel low.

"You know, you can take the test again."

"Yeah, but I gotta go to summer school! I'm still not going to be able to graduate with you guys. All the times we talked about walking across that stage together, doing something to really leave our mark on Lucy Laney. I'll just be watching from the stands. Man, that's only because I want to be in the house when you guys do your thang. I didn't want to come at all!"

"Man, you don't have to come," Cole said. "It's just a stupid piece of paper."

"Naw, man, don't even talk like that. Both of y'all work hard. Going to University of South Carolina and Georgia Tech, y'all gon' be big ballers. Let's just face it, y'all got a friend who ain't about nothing. One of us had to make the statistics about what they say about brothas true, right? I ain't never been nothing and I ain't gon' never be nothing!"

"Naw, partner, I never heard that. You got to believe that whatever dreams you have inside, you can make happen. I'm not saying it's going to be easy, but when you work through summer school, you'll be fine."

"I don't know, as crazy as Damarius is," Cole said, "he'll be in there hanging with all the honeys."

The three of us laughed.

"See, that's what I'm talking about!"

"The way you rise above, man, don't let some state-mandated test make you feel inadequate. Look at it as a challenge. If I got to sit with you and go over some stuff . . ."

"Yeah, me too! Okay, okay, don't look at me like that, D!" Cole said. "I don't know much, but whatever I know, I can help you with."

"Y'all really be in it with me?"

"Fa'sho!" we told him.

He slapped our backs together. We were all different, but we had an unbreakable bond that I knew would be there forever.

"I'm tired of working out," Damarius said.

"Man, you know we can't quit!" I told him.

"I know y'all both got training and y'all have to report to school in a little while. I'll catch up with y'all later."

When Damarius left, I went to take his place and help Cole bench-press. But he didn't lean back to lift the 400-pound bar.

"What's up? It's not too heavy for you, is it?" I teased.

"Ha, ha, ha!" Cole said back. "Naw, man, ju . . . I don't know . . . just a lot."

"Yeah, tough break about Damarius, huh? I heard them stupid tests be rigged anyway."

"What you mean, rigged? If it was rigged, he would have passed it."

"Naw, I overheard our teachers and stuff say the state looks at all the answers the black kids get right and goes in and takes those questions off the test for the next year. I mean, they trying to make it where we don't pass."

"Man, don't believe that," I said to him.

"Alright, man, you like to think we live in a perfect world. Even though they welcomed Ray Charles back, you saw the movie Jamie Foxx was in. Let's be real—at one time they didn't even want him to play because he wanted to end segregation. And that happened right here in Augusta."

"So what you gon' do, let all that make you all hot and bothered up under the collar and get nothing done?"

"I don't know. I don't know. I'm just saying, I'm about to go South Carolina, Columbia—an all-white school. I mean, aren't you nervous? We've been in the predominantly black Richland County school system all our lives, let's just talk honestly here. Keep it real! I'm used to seeing the brothers and the sisters. I don't know nothing about white people. And I'm going to have to live with some of them. Don't they get lice?"

"Boy, you so stupid!" I said as I knocked my hand up against his head. "We can get lice, too."

"School me then, tell me something."

"I don't know, maybe it's not a black or white thing with me, maybe it's just that I don't think my talent is that good. I'm just coming around to being. It was cool to be the man in our little high school, you know playing folks in our area and stuff. We were almost state. But now to take that to a college level, I've been watching some of their film and their D-line men come off the ball so hard. Can I fit into that scheme, Perry? I mean, you don't have anything to be worried about, but I do!"

Grabbing both our water bottles off the floor, I handed him his and took a swig of mine. As I let the liquid cool me down, I prayed inwardly for the Lord to give me the words to share with my friend.

"Look, I don't want you to think that I am not nervous about going to Tech. Even academically I know I am going to be challenged, so I feel you on all that. But ever since I've been talking to God, giving all my fears to Him, some way, somehow, He calms me down, and He either works my problem out or gives me the strength to survive what I gotta go through."

"So you know God is really real, huh?" Cole asked me plainly.

"Try Him. I have had peace so relaxing, man, but don't take my word for it. Ask Him to show you. Plus, you *should* be scared—you can't even bench four hundred pounds," I teased, trying to use reverse psychology.

"Awh, man, I can do this," Cole said as he leaned back, lifting up the bar with no problem.

That was my boy. Hopefully he was going to give the Lord a try. If he did, his life would never be more meaningful.

After we were done, we hit the showers. Cole had to go to his locker to get something so I walked alone to my car.

"Can I talk to you for a second?" Tori's familiar voice said from behind my back.

Dang, I did not want to turn around. That girl had caused me so many problems.

"Perry, I know you hear me. Please, just give me a second!"

Yeah, I heard her alright and that was half the problem. I didn't want to hear her; I just wanted her to leave me alone.

"I miss you, please can we talk? I know you're mad at me, but just a second. I just want to share what's in my heart, please."

Finally I turned around. I didn't want her to misread my giving her a bit of my time so I said, "Look, I'm really sorry about what you're going through. I know you still got this thing for me. And I want to say 'I care,' I don't want you to be hurt, that's for sure, but I don't know what I feel. All I can tell you is there was a time when you wanted to have sex with me. You've done that! There was a time when you wanted to make me jealous with another dude. You've done that! Shoot, you might even have wanted to make me pay because I wasn't straight up about being in another relationship or ending it, whatever. Hmm-mmm, you embarrassed the heck out of me at that debutante ball, so you've even done that! I don't know what your angle is this time, but I don't have any more to give you, Tori. I can't even say let's be friends, you know. I just need to be truthful. You need to leave me alone. Go pray or something!"

Tears started to flow from her eyes. I knew that was going to get to me. I mean, I wasn't a cold heartless dude, but I couldn't fall for any of that. I mean seriously, we had exhausted all the good stuff.

"I know I said it sort of nonchalantly about praying, but I'm serious here, Tori. You got to let God heal you. Quit clinging on to me, and move the heck on."

As I turned around slowly to walk away, I prayed, "Lord, I know she thinks I'm trying to hurt her. You know that's not the case, and if she doesn't go to you, I'm asking you to go to her. She can't be so stuck on a guy. That's just real unattractive. And I know she shouldn't keep thinking 'I'm a player,' but dang, help me so I won't look a fool either. I want you to feel me, I want you to feel her; help Cole and Damarius, too. Shucks, we all need you, we all need you bad."

Being in student government, I hadn't done much all year. With football and recruiting, no one sweated me about not putting in enough time; however, for graduation activities it was my turn to be on deck. They had me in charge of everything for the baccalaureate service; problem was no one told me until seven days before the big event. Justin and I were going over the program and I noticed there was no one's name listed as the guest speaker. When I pointed it out to him, he just started panicking.

"See, this is what I'm saying. This is why you should have been in on this a long time ago, because now it's a couple of days away and we don't have anybody to speak. Our budget's low, I mean, who are we going to be able to afford to get that's good, and you know you have to speak, too, right?"

"What you mean, I got to speak, too?"

"You're salutatorian. Valedictorian speaks at graduation, and you speak at the baccalaureate. Come on, man!"

"Are you making this up?" I asked him.

"No, he's not making it up," our superintendent startled us both by saying.

"Dr. Franklin!" I said, really excited to see one of my father's old friends.

He used to be principal at our old high school before he got a chance to get the big job.

"Perry Skky Jr., man, you doing your thang, huh? I taught you something when I was here, right?"

"Yes sir, Dr. Franklin," I said as I laughed.

Dr. Franklin was a cool old black man, but he tripped most of us out because every day he wore the same black suit. Okay, let me correct myself—not the exact same suit, but all the black suits he wore looked alike. And even though I hadn't see him in a while, it looked like that ritual had not changed.

"I see you checking out my digs. Don't get jealous—you'll get into your routine once you get in college and make that big money after school. If I look good in black like I told you a long time ago, why change it."

"Dr. Franklin, can you speak for our baccalaureate services?" I asked, knowing he'd be a perfect candidate to give some inspiring words.

"Son, I'm already going to be there, gotta dig a little deeper. You know big people in high places. You can think of somebody."

"Sir, I can't think of anybody."

"Besides a parent, who has inspired you lately?"

"That's easy. It would be the chaplain of the Georgia Tech Yellow Jackets football team. But would he do it? Would his schedule allow him to come?"

There was only one way to find out. I grabbed my cell phone and tried to step out into the hall.

Justin said, "Wait, where you going, we got to finish this thing."

"No, no, no. Just give me a second, I got an idea."

"Alright!"

I just dialed his number, which was stored in my phone. I didn't want to think about how I was going to pitch it or anything like that. Either he could do it, or he couldn't and I'd have to go back to the drawing board. I was very excited when he seemed to have some enthusiasm about hearing from me.

"Hey, Perry, man, what's going on?" Charlie Moss, the chaplain said.

"C. Moss," I said, "I hate to bother you with this."

"No, no. It's never a bother. What's going on?"

"I know it's a long shot."

"What, what are you talking about?"

"Well, we don't even have enough money."

"Son, what are you talking about? Just talk to me."

"You just inspire me a lot, and every time I hear you speak, and umm, I'm in charge of this baccalaureate program for my school and we need a speaker and . . ."

"You asking me?" he helped me get it out by saying.

"Yeah!" I replied.

"Sign me up, give me the details."

"Well, it's this coming up Sunday."

"Okay, and the time? I'm sure it's in Augusta, right?"

We talked for a few minutes, setting up everything, and I didn't even have to give him a fee.

I knew he was going to say something that would encourage us all. It was just great to know that he was willing to help me out and I wasn't even a part of his football team yet. It just went a long way to show me that he and I were going to have a great relationship; at least I could say early on if I got myself into trouble, I'd have someone to turn to. He was already proving to be a man that could help me out of a bind.

It didn't take me long to be able to thank him because the week flew by. I was actually getting a little sad that my time in high school was ending—not too sad, just a little. Because I had aced all my classes, I had no exams, so when I went to school, it was to help teachers take down their bulletin boards or put library books back on the shelf, just help out wherever I could. But now we were in Payne College's auditorium. C. Moss was there decked out in his three-piece suit. Dr. Franklin was seated up on the stage with me as well, in his—you guessed it—black suit. I could look out into the audience and see my parents beaming with pride, and as it was my time to say something inspiring to my fellow classmates, I called for the Lord's help. I mean, I didn't want to say just anything to them; I wanted to say something that would have an impact, and though I'd worked hard on my speech, I hoped what I had prepared would come out right.

"To everyone here—school administrators, parents, and my fellow classmates—I'm glad to stand before you today as this year's Lucy Laney's salutatorian. I'm glad, too, that I am not the valedictorian, because I get a chance to speak to you on a spiritual level, and this last year a lot of great things have happened to me. I'm not talking about football accomplishments. Yeah, they have been a blessing for my life, but I've grown and walked with the Lord. He doesn't always take me where I want to be, but I am certainly on a good path—I have a good foundation now because I trust God with my life. I've prepared some things to say to you, trying to quote some scriptures, stuff like that, but I figure it's better if I just talk from the heart and keep it real, so to speak. Is that all right?"

"Talk to the people now," some lady said from the audience.

"I simply have three points, and I think they will hit everyone in this room. First thing is if you don't know God, get to know Him He will change your life for the better. There is not a problem He can't fix, and even though we might still be knuckleheads once we know Him, knowing Him makes life easier. My second point is if you know Him, if you believe there is a God up in Heaven, get to know Him more. Spend more time in His word so that you can understand the path that He has for your life. Sometimes we go astray because we can't hear what He wants us to do and we can only take in the fullness of this life if we understand where He wants us to go. My last point is if you have a great relationship with Him and He is your best friend, then tell others about Him because that is our true calling in this life. Not to become the world's greatest football player, or to be the superintendent, or to pick up trash, or to do hair. All those things are great if that is your heart's desire and if that's what you feel God wants you to do. But He also calls us to win souls for Him. If you want true happiness, if you want to make the best of your life, go be a fisher of men. Greatness is awaiting us all. Let us get back together one day in Heaven, rejoicing that the Lord has said, 'Well done.' "

I got a standing ovation.

C. Moss followed me. He shook my hand before I got to sit down, and then he pulled me back to the podium with him.

"Now see, I don't have to say anything. This young man said it all."

Everyone laughed, and I thanked him for coming, and then he began giving us a charge.

"It's amazing how the Lord works in mysterious ways. Perry touched on what my message was to you guys, which is to live your life for Christ. You are high school graduates . . . almost"—the audience laughed—"seriously, let's just call tomorrow as if it was today. You are high school graduates. You've done it. You've gone on to make your parents proud, and you are leaving Lucy Laney High School. Some of you may be wondering what's next, others of you may even know what you want to do with your life, but Perry hit on it: If you give your life to the Lord, if you allow Him to direct each step of your life, you'll score touchdowns daily. You'll hear the applause from Heaven. The Lord made you for a reason, each of you can achieve greatness, but you have to give it all to Him. Pursue your dreams, but with every breath, make sure He's with you. Pray daily and know that though life won't always be easy, with the Lord by your side, it will be remarkable! Greatness awaits you! Go get it, Lucy Laney graduates!"

We all cheered, and I was thrilled to see the faces of my classmates beaming with excitement and passion and ready to go and make their dreams come true. I'd done a good thing inviting C. Moss to speak to us. He spoke from the heart, and we all received it. He gave it to us straight, and we loved him speaking it plain.

After the baccalaureate services, my mom had C. Moss come over to the house for dinner. He and my dad spent a great deal of time talking football. It was actually fun seeing the chaplain so down to earth—it got me really excited to get to Tech and get to know him more. He had an unconventional style; I mean, he was really down. It wasn't like he was cussing or anything, but I could see him jacking up a player or trying to get his point across.

"Mrs. Skky, these yams are delicious!" he said, stroking my mom just the right way.

"Well, thank you, sir. You know you are welcome back here anytime."

"We put a little extra in his food!" my dad said. "We want you to take care of our boy!"

"Oh yeah, you got a good kid here, sir," C. Moss replied. "He's going to help me handle the rest of the rookies."

"Yes, he's usually pretty responsible," my mom said, surprising even me. She talked good about me in front of company. "But . . ." she began.

Making me aware that the other shoe was about to drop.

"C'mon, Mom! Just leave it at that."

"No, son, you do need to be reminded of things from time to time."

"Like what, what?"

"Your tuxedo is due back today or you're going to have to pay a late fee. And it's Sunday. The mall will be closed shortly."

"Oh, snap!" I said, looking at the time.

I had less than an hour to get over there, but I didn't want to leave my guest. I sort of wanted to have time to dialogue with him. Then C. Moss offered to come.

"You gon' ride with that boy?" my dad joked.

"Yes, sir, it'll give us a chance to talk."

Fifteen minutes later we were headed to the mall. I looked over at the speed limit and consciously made sure I was obeying the laws. C. Moss caught my eye checking out the sign.

"So, your dad must know you pretty well. You don't follow the speed laws, huh?"

"Naw, you know I just don't remember what they are because they change so fast," I said.

"Well, son, you really did a good job today."

"Oh please, what I said was nothing. You're the one who encouraged us; I'm looking forward to having you at Tech."

"The passion that you talked about, wanting to grow in Christ like that, was that for real or were you just saying something that sounded good?" he asked surprisingly.

"Naw, I was serious about that."

"Well, what are you doing to get to know the Lord more?"

"I'm praying . . . and thinking about Him . . . and going to church. I don't know, what else should I be doing?"

"It's no set formula, but having a heart that's open to want to know how to get closer to the Lord is definitely a closer step in the right direction."

"Will you help me with that?"

"If you're open to my services, yeah. I'll be there for you when you come to school. How do you feel about that anyway?"

"I don't know. My boy is going to South Carolina and he's definitely a little nervous. I lifted him up by telling him, 'No big thing, college is just like high school,' but I remember when Coach Red came down and made sure that I was coming to Tech—he told me that it's not the same. So, I guess in some way I'm feeling the pressure. Didn't want to admit it to myself, you know, trying to stay positive."

"Admitting what is really going on deep inside you is the best way to conquer the negative stuff, because you don't have to deal with it alone. Just take it off of you and give it straight to the Lord . . .

"And know that anytime you want to talk to me, you can. We straight?"

"Yeah, appreciate that," I said to him. "Well, I'm just going to run right in, drop this tux off, and be right back. I know you need to hit the road and get on back to Atlanta."

"Yeah, my wife and my girls are waiting on me, so I'll just stay here."

When I went inside the tux shop, it wasn't going to be as easy as I thought to just turn in my suit and leave. It looked like a lot of guys had waited until the last minute to turn in their stuff. Thankfully, all you had to do was give your last name and they checked to see if everything was there and they took it. But this dude in front of me was late; it was a white dude, and his buddy was trying to talk the sweet blond salesgirl into not making them pay the penalty, which was half of what it cost to rent the tux. Nobody wanted to pay that even if you had the money—why waste forty bucks?

"C'mon. Go get the manager. Let me just talk to him. Seriously, I forgot, I didn't even look at the date. I thought I was to turn it in today, not yesterday. Please!!"

"Hold on, sir, I'll be right with you," she said as she acknowledged me.

Moments later she came back with the manager.

"Yes, sir, how can I help you? I'm Mr. Cannon, the store manager."

"Awh, Mr. Cannon, look . . . you just gotta cut me some slack. I had a little hangover, you know," the dude in front of me said to the white manager. "Please don't make me pay forty bucks. Half of my school came in here and got a tux. Help me out!"

He looked and saw that no one was in line behind me. "All right, I don't do this for just anybody. We'll let you slide today. Thank you for your business."

It wasn't like I cared that the guy got a break. One day late, mmm, why should he have to pay the extra money anyway? I know my mom said I needed to be more responsible, and if she hadn't reminded me, I probably would be in the same boat. So I was glad the manager okay'd it. Never thought it would even come up again. I turned in my tux, had more fun with C. Moss, and before I knew it, it was the next day.

I woke up early to Damarius asking for a favor. "What, guy, I ain't even have to go to class. No exams, I don't have an exam for P.E. either," Damarius told me.

"What's up? What you want?"

"Oh see, now you don't have time for your little ol' friends who didn't make the cut."

"Oh naw, don't even play me like that. What you want?"

"I didn't turn in my tux and it was due yesterday. I didn't even want to go to prom fooling with you and Cole."

"Alright, alright. No problem."

"Man, I don't have no extra money. I need some dollars to turn this thing in."

"Naw, naw. They'll take it back."

"How you know? They'll never take it back."

"I was in there yesterday. This dude was right in front of me. The manager, his name is Mr. Cannon, seriously, he'll take it back. C'mon, no sweat! I'll pick you up at nine thirty, we'll be there at ten when they open."

"All right, cool!"

Mr. Cannon was definitely in the shop bright and early. I was all smiles and hinted to my boy Damarius that that was the dude who was going to take care of it with no problem.

Damarius said, "Here's my tux, man. Sorry I'm late. Just need a little break."

The manager looked at the two of us and said, "And I need the late fee! Forty bucks!"

I couldn't believe he was tripping like that. I mean, I had just seen this man yesterday and he had cut the white boy some slack. I didn't want to make everything a black-and-white issue, but for real, why couldn't he not let my boy have any drama? When I saw he wasn't going to work it out, I stepped in and said, "Look, Mr. Cannon, I was in here yesterday at five forty-nine and I was the last customer in here and I had to wait while the salesgirl went to the back and got you. And this white boy who was only a day late, you let him slide. I think his exact words were, 'Half my school comes in here and uses your place,' or something like that. So, umm, now that we're black, you're not going to give us the same courtesy. I've rented four tuxedos from you and turned the last one in yesterday. I don't have a problem bad-mouthing this place.

"My boy is not paying, right?"

He looked me up and down, not believing that this black boy had him cornered.

"Oh yes, I remember you," he said finally. "For special customers I do wave the fee, and since you're with this gentleman who rented so many tuxes from us, I extend an apology. No need to pay more."

Damarius and I left the place with steam coming out of our ears. I just couldn't believe we had been treated differently because of our color.

"What the heck was that about?" Damarius tried to give me props, slapping my hands and everything.

I wasn't feeling that I was cool; I just demanded what was right. I knew the manager could overlook the late policy, though I got up there yesterday on time because I wanted to adhere to his rules. But when I saw him give a white customer special favors, then I only wanted the same for my boy. Right was right, and wrong was wrong. I just needed the man to make this good, and thankfully he did.

"Man, you called a spade a spade, you made that white man turn red. I know he was hot; he had to let me off the hook."

"I didn't do nothing big. I was just speaking it plain."

~ 3 ~

Walking with Pride

"Okay, so who's the white chick walking across your diving board, Perry?" Damarius said, drooling over my biracial cousin.

It was Memorial Day, and my family had gotten in town for my graduation, which would be taking place tomorrow. All the relatives were up from my father's side, though my mother was an only child and she and her parents had a strained relationship. I never quite understood why, but they lived down in Mobile, Alabama, and I never saw my maternal grandparents much. Damarius and Cole had come over for steaks and hot dogs, when my boy couldn't keep his eyes off my flirtatious cousin. I remember when she came to live with us two summers ago; Velar and Payton got into many female spats. She even came on to Dakari, Payton's ex, and because my sister wasn't over the guy, the two had trouble coexisting. I always thought Payton was exaggerating when she said Velar made herself too available to guys, but even I had to do a double take as my cousin jumped high in the air, and as she noticed an audience watching her, she somehow managed to let her swimsuit top come off.

"Oh, snap!" Damarius said. "Dang, she's fine!"

"Boy, my uncle Percy is around here, and trust me when I say he will jack you up about messing with his daughter."

"So her mom's white?"

"Duh, man!" Cole said, messing with him.

"Perry, can you hand me my towel?" my cousin called out as she blushed at my boys.

"Awh, man, I'm sorry, but look. I hadn't been feelin' anybody since Ciara. I mean, let's just be real about it. I miss my girl."

"I know, man," I said as I put my hand on the back of my friend.

It still was hard for me to take that his girl had died in a car accident months before, but even though he had my sympathy, I wasn't about to let him practice getting back in the saddle with my cousin. Mmm-mmm. But even though I was there giving both of them crazy looks, it was like I wasn't even there. After I handed my cousin the towel, she swung her long hair from side to side to turn my boy on. I went over to her and said, "Listen, go upstairs and put on some clothes."

She and I really didn't know each other that well, and although my cousin had an innocent look on her face, she was also a little witch. She rolled her eyes at me like I was stopping her from her game or something.

Cunningly she said, "Listen, I had to come here for your graduation. My mom and dad made me. So don't think I'm here not to have any fun. I planned to make this trip worthwhile for me—introduce me to your friend now."

"That's right, man, introduce us." Damarius came into the conversation uninvited.

"Back up, D, she needs to go change."

My cousin extended her hand and accidentally let her towel slip. I was appalled because I knew it wasn't an accident at all. I got in front of her and looked both my buddies in the face.

"C'mon y'all, she needs some privacy for real. My cousin

needs to get dressed. My dad comes out here and sees her . . . C'mon y'all."

But Damarius was just trying to get a peek and Velar was skinnin' and grinning behind me.

"C'mon, man, the girl needs to get dressed," Cole finally told Damarius as he pulled him over by the grill.

"Alright, alright! I'll lay off, I'll get back, but when your dad gon' start cooking? I'm hungry."

"Boy, would I like to feed you!" Velar said in a voice only I could hear.

I was so mad at her. Why did she think the whole come-on thing was attractive?

"Being real," I said. "You sound like a slut."

She raised her hand and slapped me in the face. At that point I didn't care what she did.

"I'm sorry, Perry. I'm sorry!"

"Whatever, Velar. Whatever."

I walked away, and Velar picked up her towel and ran inside.

"Dang, boy, what did you say to your cousin?" Cole asked.

But I didn't respond. There was no need to go into all of that. I didn't want to go into that with either one of them, but Cole kept ragging me.

"I guess you gotta let your cousin hit you like that," he said. Damarius laughed.

Thankfully I didn't have to keep going on and on about it because my relatives came outside.

"Perry, what did you and your boys do to Velar? She ran up the stairs," my uncle Percy said.

"Naw, sir. We didn't really talk to her," Damarius cut in and replied. "But you have a lovely daughter." He extended his arm to my uncle.

Uncle Percy wasn't a fool, though we didn't spend that

much time together because he and his wife, Maggie, lived out in Colorado. He was still fully aware of what a lie sounded like.

"Uh-huh!" he replied as he looked my partner up and down.

"I'm his boy Damarius, umm, we've been friends for years."

"Oh, so you're graduating, too, huh?"

Damarius didn't know how to respond to that. Cole and I wanted to have his back; we didn't want him to be embarrassed or anything.

So I said, "Umm, uh, this is my other friend, Cole. He's going to the University of South Carolina."

"Oh yeah, my school," my uncle told him, forgetting all about the question he'd asked Damarius. Damarius got lost in the crowd. I introduced Cole to my two aunts: Georgia and Rebecca. It was funny—though they had both grown up in Georgia, when they became adults, one aunt moved to New Jersey and the other one moved to Texas. My dad was the baby of the four of them and there was a little sibling rivalry when my grandfather left my dad in charge of the estate. I don't know why they were surprised, though; my dad had been running the dealership when my grandfather retired. Naturally, the two of them had a bond, but when money got involved, it could make family turn into enemy. Add to that the fact that they didn't have the best relationship in the first place, and I was really surprised the three of them were here to support me.

"My little nephew is growing up," said my aunt Rebecca, who had no children. "Boy, I remember changing your diapers, and pretty soon you'll be going across the stage and getting a diploma. Look at you!"

My aunt Georgia from Texas had two grown sons.

"How are your boys doing?" I asked her.

"Boy, don't ask about them. They are double your age and still living in my house. I don't know why most men are so trifling and lazy."

That was an interesting comment. I had heard it before, and as a young black man, I took offense to it. Even though there were a lot of us in jail, not wanting to work, abusive, or dead way too young, there were still a lot of us who were holding things down, taking care of our family, continuing our education, and contributing positively to society. That people focused more on the negative was something I hoped would change, but I was smart enough to know not to take up that battle with my aunt. She was too set in her ways and apparently too upset with her children. Not a battle for me to fight that day. I looked around and realized Damarius wasn't anywhere. My dad hadn't gotten back from the dealership so I knew my friend couldn't be talking to him, and my mom was outside with my aunts, so I dismissed even the small possibility that he'd be a gentleman and help her bring things out. My cousin wasn't around either so I went inside and headed up to Payton's room, where Velar was staying.

"Oh, heck naw!" I said, standing in the doorway of my sister's room.

I saw my cousin and my friend with their tongues down each other's throats.

"Oh, man, Perry, I just came up here to use the restroom and . . . and . . ."

"Man, leave my house!" I said forcefully.

"You don't have to ask him to leave if you don't want him to be your company; he's over here hanging out with me! My mom's inside, she doesn't mind. Plus I'm in college. I can do what I want to do."

"Your mom's in the shower, Velar."

"Dude, leave, man. Seriously."

"Awh, man, Perry, you gon' act like that? Whatever, man, she ain't kiss that good noway."

My cousin reached for a pillow off Payton's bed and threw it toward the door, hitting Damarius in the back of the head.

I knew if I said something to her, she might start crying like a little baby or retaliate, hitting us again. Neither one of these could I tolerate so I just walked out of the room, shaking my head and wondering if she had any honor.

Before I could get down the stairs, my cousin followed me and said, "Wait, Perry, please. I just want to talk to you."

The tone in her voice was a switch. It wasn't so defensive and I didn't mind explaining why I was upset about seeing her in the arms of my player best friend.

"Alright, c'mon," I said as I motioned for her to follow me. We went into the family room and I waited for her to begin.

"Clearly your friend is a jerk and then as he left he made a bad comment about me being a bad kisser. What was I thinking?"

That was a good question for her to ask herself, 'cause I was certainly wondering the same thing and I had no answers for her.

"I guess I wasn't using my head and you tried to tell me. I mean, outside you practically ordered me to leave him alone and maybe that's what made me disobey you. You know, I mean, my dad was so protective for years and I'm finally in college. Gotten through my first year and I'm still trying to find myself."

"What do you mean by that?" I wasn't sure about what the heck she was talking about.

"I go to UCLA, a predominantly white school. I've dated tons of guys, Perry, and I've not found someone that connects with me."

"Maybe you just haven't found the right guy."

"Most of the people I'm around are white, and I don't know, a part of me isn't white. Maybe I'm not connecting because I need to be dating a black guy, what do you think?"

Of course I would say dating a black guy would be the

smartest thing she could ever do. She'd be dating someone like her dad, someone like her cousin—me. I was definitely tired of everyone thinking, "White is right." But I couldn't respond with how I felt, since this wasn't my life.

"You gotta say something. I mean you basically telling me not to talk to your boy, was it because he was a black guy and all black guys are dogs or something?"

"Cuz, I didn't mean to call you names and stuff like that, but you just come across a little too forceful, like you're ready to give it up. If that's your approach, whether the guy is black, white, Chinese, Oriental, biracial, he's not going to respect you. Some things transcend color. I hadn't figured it out, shoot I got females problems myself. But I know I'm running far away from those girls just throwing themselves at me, not respecting any element of themselves. The last thing I want is for you to be with the wrong guy, and though I know my boy 'D' will show you a good time, he showed his true colors. He was only after one thing. I just want you to have the best, that's all. Don't sell yourself short."

"Thanks, cuz," she said. "Please don't tell Payton this when she comes home tonight. She and I have had this conversation before, but I think hearing it from you, I don't know, it's just sinking in more."

"I got you. It's just between us."

"Velar, hand me that bag in the guest room," her mom called from the bathroom. When she strolled out, she gave me a thumbs-up. I was excited to see that she got it. When I got outside, Damarius was trying to get Cole to stop eating the barbeque.

"Man, I just got here. I ain't going nowhere. You and Perry need to go and work that out," Cole said to him.

"C'mon, man, let's go," Damarius said as he grabbed Cole's plate and put a napkin over it.

"Boy, you will get stomped in front of Perry's family. You

better put my plate down. I'm hungry and I done helped his uncle fix this nice meal," Cole said. "Perry, you better come get your boy."

"Dang," Damarius replied as he walked in the opposite direction.

"Man, wait. Can I talk to you?" I was glad that my mom and my aunts were inside now.

I knew Damarius was a hothead and I certainly didn't want either of them to see us go at it.

"Oh, so you ain't gon' stop? You just gon' keep walking away from me?"

"That's what it looks like. You getting the diploma tomorrow. Figure it out."

"So that's what this is about. You mad at me because I'm getting a diploma and you not, or you mad because I stopped you from using my cousin."

Damarius turned and said, "News flash, man, the chick wanted to give it up to me. I ain't have to work at all to get that. Just because you still trying to be the choir boy don't mean that's the angle I'm trying to take."

"Yeah, man, but every time you don't get your way, you sit there and pout or insult people. Am I right or wrong—you ain't care about her? Why would I want my cousin to get screwed like that?"

"Looks like she's a big enough girl. She can figure it out for herself. You having a party and all that showing off that you graduating, that you big time in the class—summa cum laude. You're such a show-off, man."

I walked three steps in my friend's face and said, "I'm not summa cum anything. I'm salutatorian because I did my work, got the right grades for it to fall like that. Your tail always wants to eat a free meal. So my folks are throwing this little cookout. We got family in town and all I did was invite you and Cole over. He don't seem to be having no problem with it."

"Yeah, 'cause he just happy to be in your company. I'm not your little pawn, though, dude. You and your cousin can go to he—"

"Wait, though, dude." I could hardly say it. "Why it gotta be like that?"

"You weren't in the school thing. You were the one that chose to hang with Jayboe, running with the wrong crowds and getting high and stuff. You couldn't know anything about school with your brain all fried. And as soon as teams started losing interest in you on a college level, you acted like getting a high school diploma was beneath you."

"I don't need no lecture from you. Get out of my dang-on way. Tell Cole I'll be at the car."

"Naw, dude, can't do. Do it yourself."

"Be like that then." Throwing up his hands, my frustrated friend didn't say goodbye to anyone, but made a scene leaving as he kicked up the grass and banged the trash can on the way out.

Cole came over and said, "Man, let me get out of here and take him home. Don't even worry about it. He just mad because he won't have that piece of paper tomorrow."

"Well, why he got to be mad at me because I'm getting mine, you know?"

"You know your boy!"

"Alright, partner, see ya."

We slapped hands and Cole was gone, but not, of course, without his food. I took off my T-shirt and dived in the pool. I certainly needed to cool off. Damarius had gotten to me. I knew he was hurting, but I couldn't just let him walk over me and think that was okay. When I did the backstroke, my uncle called out, "Mind if I join you?"

"No sir," I said as he splashed into the water.

"So your little friend is mad at you, huh?"

"Oh, so you saw his exit?"

"Yeah, I saw it. I understand it, too."

"Sir?" I said, unaware of where this talk was going.

"Son, sometimes you don't know how to respond when someone you love is getting more than you, and you retaliate the wrong way. I'm sure you know I was very disappointed when my dad left the dealership to your father. I still get a little hustle out of it, but I don't run it."

"You don't have to tell me none of this, Uncle Percy."

"Oh no, I do. My wife helped me get straight. Telling me I was jealous and that I was setting the wrong example for my children. My brother did what he was supposed to do. He learned the business. I was out running the streets, so when it came time for Dad to give it to someone, your dad was ready. And though I should have been mad at myself, I shouldn't have been angry at him. So I can understand where your friend is coming from. He's really mad at himself; he doesn't know how to express it so he's taking it out on you."

"How am I supposed to respond?" I asked, being that he had way more insight into this behavior than I did.

"You can't let him get away with it." He had taken the words right out of my mouth. "But you can't push it in his face either. He'll come around, pray him through it, call him out on his faults, but be willing to have a forgiving spirit. Because in a day he will realize he is tripping, and when he comes back into your life with an apology, don't hold it over his head!"

"Yes, sir."

"Your dad didn't with me and now I can enjoy my nephew's graduation. You know I'm proud of you, son. I know it's got to be tough, all the pressure on you with the whole football thang. Know you got fans clear cross the country and I believe

Damarius is a good friend of yours, and as you keep climbing the ladder of success, you gon' need those types of people around you, so again, cut him some slack. He'll come around."

My uncle and I slapped hands, and then he wanted to race me to the other side of the pool. Of course, I had to let him win.

I woke up the morning of my graduation humbled. So many times I'd thought about this day, not just graduating with honors but having a college scholarship waiting for me. Though I had asked the Lord to help make each day more meaningful, he'd answered in a mighty way and that really made me proud. I wasn't going to be overly emotional. For two years it had just been me and my folks since Payton was away at college. The house usually seemed quiet, but today it wasn't like that. Grandmother had already called me four times to come down and eat her spread, and though my aunts wanted to stay in a hotel, my parents wouldn't have it any other way. So they were there as well as my uncle Percy and his wife and daughter, all under one roof for me. When I got to the table all decked in my suit, anxiously waiting to put on my robe and get the show over with, I was greeted by plenty of hugs and kisses.

"Awh, my baby. He's graduating!" my grandmother said as she kissed me.

I whispered in her ear, "You not high now, are you?" She slapped me on the head and said, "Alright, boy, don't get too grown."

"I'm just playing, Grandma," I said, sort of playing and sort of really wanting to check to make sure she was okay.

"So if the football thing don't work out, what you gon' do, son?" Uncle Percy asked.

I guess Dad took it as a slap in the face, their little sibling rivalry starting to gear up.

"He gon' do the same thing your son's doing, work hard to try and get a job."

"Awh, see now. Why you got to act like that? I was just teasing with the boy. He ain't take it the wrong way. Why you got to take it the wrong—"

"Boys, calm down!" my grandmother said.

"Yeah, for real, Dad, he's just playing. It's cool!"

My aunt Maggie said to her husband, "See, I don't know why you even getting your brother started."

"It ain't my fault he can't take a joke. Just so you know, little brother, your son and I talked the other day. He doesn't just want to sell cars; he wants to design them."

"You do, son?" my dad said as he turned his frown into a smile.

"Yeah, I'm thinking about taking up mechanical engineering."

"Son, that's wonderful," my dad said to me as he came over to me and gave me a big hug.

"I'm sorry, Percy. I didn't know you two talked. I just thought you were trying to give me a hard time as usual. It's like I never could measure up to your shoes."

"What are you talking about? I was telling your son yesterday how, though I'm the big brother, I admire you. You raised a good son here. Dad would be real proud."

I missed my grandfather and at that moment his two sons were bonding. I took a second to reflect; my grandfather had taught me a lot. He'd always wanted to be able to see me graduate from high school but he fell a little short of that goal. Yet I believe he was up in Heaven telling everyone, "That's my boy." And as my family settled back down and ate Grandma's pancakes, sausage, grits, and corn beef hash, though we knew we were missing the monarch, we could hold our heads up high knowing we were doing him right. Because Grandma wouldn't let anybody up from the table until everybody was done, it was time to head to the school as soon as the meal ended. They wanted me to ride in the car with them but I was thankful I was able to head out in my own ride; turning on some dance music, I was able to mellow out and continue reflecting. A part of my life was almost over, and though I'd waited for this moment, I was a little melancholy. No longer could I depend on my folks to supply my needs; I had to be more responsible and really start taking care of me.

Looking up at the sun, I prayed, "Lord, I am so thankful for today. I don't know why you have blessed me so. I certainly know I don't deserve any of it. But because you have given me a lot, Lord, I want to honor you with each and every one of the rest of my days. So many things I don't understand: inequality, injustice, and why people say a black man has it so hard—hearing stuff like that can make it a little difficult for me to want to be real excited about tomorrow. I can put aside the strife of the world and concentrate on knowing that you got my feet. Thank you again, Lord, for restoring your grace upon me. I love you and again I say 'Thank you.' In Jesus' name, Amen."

"Boy, where you been, we all lined up," Cole said to me.

I filed in line with the rest of the 149 seniors. We were expecting 172, but everyone couldn't be in that number. And as salty as I was at Damarius for being a butthead, a part of me didn't want to go through this ceremony without him.

"Skky, come here," I heard Damarius's familiar voice say. Before it was actually time for us to walk out, I got out of line and walked over to him. "Um, um . . . mmm."

He couldn't seem to find the words to say. I stuck out my hand for him to give me five.

"We cool," I said to him. "You don't have to say nothing."

"Naw, man, but I do," he said as he came out of our embrace. "I love you, man. You like a brother to me. You ain't never done me wrong, always helped even when you knew it wasn't the right thing to do. You've been there for me. I don't know why I continue to trip and do stupid stuff. And though it's real hard to be up in here seeing you and Cole getting your papers and all, I really wouldn't be able to live with myself if I missed this moment. Because today ain't about me. You're right—I didn't take care of what I needed to, to make sure I could graduate, but I ain't gon' give up on me. I'm a get it right this summer. Today is about you and Cole. So after this, I have one question."

"What's that?" I said, laughing.

"Where are we going to celebrate?"

"Hey, man, I'm a let you hook it up," I said to him, knowing that was a little dangerous, but feeling he'd step up to the challenge and have some place I didn't need to be.

"You gon' trust me to work it out? A'ight, a'ight! I got this, I got this. Party at Perry's place after graduation!"

"Boy, you stupid!" I said to him. "He was just playing," I called out.

"Naw, for real. Maybe the three of us could just take in a movie or something. Watch some old highlight films from South Carolina and Georgia Tech. Get y'all ready for what's next, boys' night out. Is that cool?"

"It's cool. Oh and I saw your cousin—I apologized."

"Thanks, man."

"Thank you for not telling me to get the heck out of your face."

"Boy, please, you said it—we brothers."

The processional music started and a teacher hollered for me to get moving. The outdoor ceremony had perfect weather; the wind was blowing across my face just enough. It was like the Lord saying, *Feel how proud of you I am?* No one wanted a long ceremony, but we were all looking forward to Dr. Franklin's address to us. Now not only was he witty, but he was a man of character. We knew he cared for us. When we were freshmen, he was our principal, and now that he was superintendent, we felt honored that he was giving us words of wisdom.

"Yep, that's right. Y'all see me looking good in this suit! Black suit!" Everyone cracked up. "But today I feel I'm looking extra special because I've got my head up, I'm feeling good on the inside, because, kids, I knew you could make it through four years of high school and come out as leaders, and you have proven to do just that."

As he talked, he had our full attention. No one was making crazy noises. He went on to say, "I'm standing up here to tell you the truth. Life from this point on is not going to be a bed of roses. You have to work hard for what you want, and you have to keep your goals in front of you and work toward something. Don't let anybody tell you that you can't! And don't take handouts—strive to be twice as good as the next guy. Don't focus on disappointments; let the negativity fuel you toward greatness. If you remember any of these things that I am telling you now, I'll see you back here in a few years and you can show me your successes. Hats off to you, class. Lucy Laney is proud."

What seemed like a long thirty minutes later, the principal said, "Perry Moss Skky Jr."

The place erupted in cheering. The adrenaline I felt was as real as if I'd run the winning touchdown in the state championship game. I stepped on that podium, shook the principal's hand, took my diploma, smiled at the audience, then moved off the podium walking with pride.

~ 4 ~

Seeing No Color

Summer was officially here. I was a high school graduate, and I was on top of the world. If I wasn't in the gym getting my knee in shape, I was running to keep up my conditioning. Damarius, Cole, and I were spending a lot of time together going to others' graduations and ironically helping my boy study for his Georgia Entrance Exam.

"I don't want to take that thing again," he said, whining at first when I told him we weren't going to just keep playing because we had to do some work as well.

"In a couple of weeks neither Cole nor I will be here, and you will be back in summer school. Do you want our help or not?"

"Alright, alright, alright!" Damarius finally let down his resistance.

And once we got into studying, we made it fun; we used chemistry examples and things he could relate to, and when it came time to go back to the basics with grammar, the adjectives and adverbs we used to describe a torn-up car made him quickly understand how to pick out the describing words. After we finished a lesson, Damarius wanted to head out and play ball. Though a game of basketball was certainly a good form of exercise, I wanted to hit the pool. Shoot, it was hot in Augusta.

"Naw, man, I'm a head home," I said to him.

"You going home to go swimming, ain't you?"

"So what, man, if I do?" I said to him. "You play ball every day."

"A'ight, a'ight. We straight. Your pool should be an ocean, though. You can just keep going and going and then maybe you'd be tired of it."

"Ha, ha, ha," I said to him.

"Well, come on, Cole, let's go shoot some hoops."

"Naw, naw, bruh. I got to go with Briana. She getting all emotional, sad knowing that I'm about to leave in a minute; I got to get my time in with her, you know."

"A'ight, cool. Y'all just leave me then."

"Awh, don't trip. You about to be doing some big things."

"You think, Perry?" Damarius said, seeing no pot of gold at the end of his rainbow.

He had been working really hard to make sure when he took the test again that he passed it, but there was no guarantee, and I couldn't give him any assurance other than the fact that I believed in him and I needed him to believe in himself.

"You can do it."

"Yeah, I can!"

Thinking I would have the pool all to myself, I was a little disappointed to find my sister and her beau splashing water on each other. I mean, they had water going every which way, and it wouldn't surprise me if they didn't stop and there wouldn't be any water left in the pool anyway. Payton was an athlete, too, and a cheerleader, and you would think the two of them would have been sensitive enough to see me there and get out of the way. But they were so into themselves that they didn't even look up. They actually drew me into their connection, and as much fun as I was having this summer, I was really missing something. I hadn't spoken to Savoy all week, and seeing them splash around in the pool, I realized it wouldn't be so bad if Savoy could enjoy the water with me.

As soon as I took a few steps away from the pool, Tad said, "Wait, partner, you ain't got to leave on our part. Payton, calm down. Your brother is trying to get a workout in."

"Yeah, right. He can come back some other time."

"It's cool," I said, knowing that my sister was a trip.

"Y'all do ya thing."

"Wait, Payton, hold up," Tad told her. "Perry, come here."

I went back over to the side of the pool.

"You know my cousin missed you at graduation last week."

With all the places my boys and I crashed, we didn't go to Silver Bluff's big day. A part of the reason was I didn't think Savoy wanted me to ruin her special moment, but hearing her cousin say that she wanted me there was all the more reason to let me know I needed to call her.

"Thanks, man," I said, giving him dap. "Is she around?"

"I don't know, man. I came here straight from Athens. I hadn't even been home yet."

"My sister keeps you on a short leash, boy."

"Ha, yeah, right. I want to be kept, remember that. I don't want to go around looking long-faced like you."

"I hear you."

"Seriously, Perry, go call her."

I agonized about thirty minutes over whether or not I actually should. Last time we were together at the hotel at the pavilion, she told me she needed space. She hadn't picked up the phone to call me; I graduated just like she did. Why did I have to be the one who reached out?

" 'Cause you were the nut who messed up!" I said to myself.

The phone rang four times, and just about when I was going to hang up and not leave a message, she said, "Hello?"

I leaned back on my bed and wished she was near me. The sound of her voice did something to me.

"Hey, it's Perry."

"Yeah, I see your number. What's going on? Long time no hear from."

"Yeah, I just had a lot to do with graduation and all. Congrats to you."

She paused. "Yeah, congrats to you, too."

"So you had a lot of family down. Tad told me."

"Yeah, it was a lot of family. Not a lot of friends, though, but it was cool."

"I would've come, but I didn't get an invite. I didn't want your dad or cousin beating me up or anything."

She finally laughed and said, "You so silly!"

I hoped I had broken the ice between us.

"Look, let me just be real. I know you said you needed some time and I respect that, I really do, but I miss you, girl. Can we hang out some?"

Again there was a long pause. Was she trying to make me sweat, or was she trying to analyze if I was telling the truth? It was like she was holding up a big stop sign, and I wanted her to give me a green light to let me know she missed me, too. For us to set up time for her to come swim with me. Why couldn't we splash around like Payton and Tad? But I didn't push.

"I understand if you're busy. I just thought maybe since I didn't make it to your graduation, I could take you out now to celebrate."

"Perry, we've always been honest with each other and I miss you, too. I don't know what really lies ahead for you and me, but I still want us to be friends. I'm busy today and tomorrow I got to babysit my cousin."

"For real, you not just pulling my leg?"

"Naw, I got to babysit my cousin. But in a couple of days you call me back and we can work out something. It'd be good to see you."

"You sound really good, though."

"I am good. Things aren't like I planned them, you know, but I'm dealing."

Her strength was attractive. Unlike Tori, she didn't need me to survive, and a part of that throwaway attitude was what made me want her to want me around. For now I'd have to settle for a date and having something cool to look forward to. I figured I'd spare no expense. I wanted to make sure she knew I really did care.

"So are we still on for today, Miss Savoy?" I said into the receiver as I talked to the girl I couldn't wait to take out. I had a lot to make up for so I had a fun day planned out for us. I had also planned a special night—I was going to take her to Howard's Barbeque. It was the region's best and the owner of Howard's was a good family friend. He had set a table for two in a small quiet room, where we would be away from his other patrons. There was one drive-in movie left in Augusta and I was planning to take her there for dessert. I had packed some candles, strawberries, whipped cream, and sparkling cider. All I needed to do was for Savoy to confirm we were still on. I would jump in the shower, dab a little cologne behind my ears, head to pick her up, and let the rest of the evening turn into magic. But she was hesitating. Was the date off? Did she not want to spend time with me?

"We're still on, right?" I probed. "I've gone through a lot of trouble—"

"Trouble?" she cut me off, then said, "Well, listen, I didn't ask you to jump through hoops for me. The whole date-again thing was your idea, Perry."

"No, no. I didn't mean it that way."

"I don't know. Maybe we shouldn't even start this up again."

"We just said we were going to be friends, so what's the harm in that? I'm on my way to pick you up."

"No, absolutely not!" she said, immediately cutting off my plans. "I want to drive and meet you somewhere."

"Why do you want to do that?"

"What, is that a problem?"

"I just wanted to treat you special; you know, come and pick you up so you can see the gentleman I can be."

"Well, that's not necessary. We can meet and I'm sure I'll see the real you. How about the mall in an hour? I'll check the movies and decide what we can see then we can eat in the food court later."

I didn't reply at first.

"Perry? Is that cool with you, or do you want to cancel the whole thing?"

"Well, if it's got to be on your terms or nothing, do I have a choice?"

I had to admit I was a little salty. I had taken time to set everything up. Howard had promised us a special table after I'd put a few dollars in his hand. My mom had helped me pack a nice picnic basket and made me hear her lecture about being careful. Was all this for nothing? Savoy didn't even want to hear what I had set up for us? My ego was bruised, but then I realized I couldn't just see things my way. This wasn't a black-or-white issue in which she'd adhere to my way or nothing. I could be flexible. I mean, what if this was third and twenty-five and they had two guys on me? I had to get them off me, be creative, and be able to catch the ball and make the first down. I was up for that task; why wasn't I up for letting the girl I liked take the lead some? I could do that, so I agreed to her terms.

"Cool," she said.

She told me we'd meet up in an hour, but I know that the clocks of some women fly a little faster when they want to make a brother sweat, so I was there fifteen minutes early. I was all smiles when she didn't show up at first, even when she was five minutes late. But when she was fifteen minutes late, I started to wonder if the chick had stood me up or not. So I dialed her digits, but it went straight to voice mail. I waited. When five more minutes passed, I got the voicemail again. I was about to leave her a message saying I was out and then I saw her car pull up to where she'd told me to meet her. Trying to stay cool, I thought at least she was okay,

"Just act like it's no big deal, Perry. Don't trip," I told myself.

"You weren't waiting long, were you?" she said sarcastically, as if my time didn't matter.

"Naw, I got here when you asked me to, but I've been on the cell phone. I haven't been keeping up with the time." Though she was the only person I called. Since she and I didn't speak, there was no reason not to play with her just a little. Now I knew I'd have her mind wondering who I was talking to on the cell phone. She was trying to be so independent so when I walked up to the movie theater to buy our tickets, I paused, seeing if she was going to pull her wallet out of her purse, be the big dog and pay for our date. But she didn't.

I chuckled. "You're a trip!"

"What, you didn't expect me to pay for it," she stated, giving me a stern look.

As I was opening the door for her, I said, "You're the one who invited me out."

"Yeah, but you changed up stuff. I didn't know what I was doing! I have to go to the ladies' room," she said.

I thought to myself, "Dang, girl you just got here." It was like she wanted to do everything in the world to upset me.

She wasn't being her usual self, I didn't know what to think, she didn't tell me that she wanted a snack, so I guess I was supposed to imagine what she was thinking. Since we'd been to the movies a few times before, I knew she liked popcorn, Raisinettes, and a Coke. The sweet and salty mixture I just couldn't figure out, but how ironic it mirrored her current attitude. She was sweet enough to come yet she made me feel this was the last place she wanted to be. Then all of a sudden the cutest mocha-colored chic wearing the cutest fro said, "Why in the world do all the fine brothers go for the light-skinned chics?"

I wanted to tell her as crazy as my girl was acting I wouldn't mind leaving with her, but I knew I couldn't be crazy so I said, "Naw, I don't discriminate like that. I can admit that I'm not into the white thing but I take sisters in all shapes, sizes, and colors."

"Okay, so there's a sister over there weighing about three hundred pounds stuffin' her face with cotton candy, you don't mind getting with her either?"

"Oh see, why you gonna tease me like that?"

"I'm just seeing if you're a brother of your word."

"Well, looking at the way she's eating that cotton slow and sticky around her mouth, she got potential."

"Oh, you're crazy. I'm Dawn. What's your name?"

"Perry."

"Perry Skky Jr., from Lucy Laney."

Why did everyone in town have to know me? Sometimes I just wanted to be invisible, but she'd already caught me stretching the truth some.

"Yeah, that's me."

She took out some lipstick, wrote her number on the back of a receipt, and stuck it in my jean pocket.

"Don't worry, it's smudge proof. When you're sick of the want-to-be-white girl, give a real sister a call. I'll show you how us dark-skinned girls run with the ball—no pun intended."

"Next!" the counter lady said thankfully.

When Dawn got her food, she waved at me in a very mannish way. How come it had to be the same time Savoy was coming out?

"See, I don't even understand you. I go to the bathroom for a few seconds and you're flirting with people. I don't even know why I was stupid enough to give this thing a try again."

"Look," I said to her as I got out of the long line I had waited in, "she just asked me what color girls I liked."

"Not the light-skinned/dark-skinned thing again?" she said as she knew what the girl had asked me. "Some light-skinned girls hate me because the texture of my hair is curly and some dark-skinned girls have a problem because of my skin color. I just wanted to have a nice evening with you. I didn't want to deal with this bull crap, but it seems wherever I go, you attract more attention than my brother."

"Well, you can't let any of that get to you, and I don't know what's got you so off balanced, but even I've been wondering what's going on with you?"

"What do you mean?' she said, all testy. "What you see is what you get. You've made me this way Perry, either you like it or not."

At that moment I realized that I didn't know what I felt for her. Yeah, I had hurt her some and I was willing to overcome whatever I needed for her to give me a chance again, but now I didn't even know if that was worth it. In front of me was just a girl who was sort of blah. We went through the motions of going on a date, but as soon as the movie was over, I told her I was tired, and waited for her to get in her car and jetted home.

* * *

"Are you Perry Skky Jr.?" a scrawny little white boy asked me after I had just parked in the Georgia Tech parking deck.

Behind him were two other guys. One of them was just as short and small while the other one towered over both of them dramatically. When the chaplain asked me to go to Hilton Head and told me I wouldn't have to drive all the way to South Carolina, I'd be able to ride with some of the other Tech players, I never thought he meant a bunch of white boys and rejects at that. I mean, I didn't know the guys but they looked like they were wannabes, not even walk-on material; riding five hours south with them was not going to be fun. Hoping these guys would take me to the guys I was supposed to be riding with, I introduced myself, "Hi, I'm Perry Skky Jr. and I'm supposed to be meeting some guys to ride down to Hilton Head with."

"Oh yeah, that's us. I'm A.J. Turkarst."

"Wait, your name sounds familiar."

"I'm the team's kicker."

The other short guy extended out his hand. "I'm Billy Dorn, punter."

And the larger guy even taller than me said, "I'm Crosby Fuller, long snapper."

Okay, they seemed nice enough, wanted to help me put my stuff into their car, asking me about the ride down, even asking was I ready for the beach, but I mean this had to be a joke, I mean, where were the brothers? The chaplain, Charlie Moss, was black. I thought we had an understanding. I thought he knew me well enough to know that I wouldn't be comfortable in this environment. Then I thought, wait—maybe I could just ride down with Charlie.

"Do you know where Coach Moss is?"

"He's not coming 'til later. He's coming with his family. Everything okay? Did you forget something? We can stop on the way to get what you need," the A.J. kid said again, being overfriendly.

He was trying to make me feel comfortable but that was not what I was about. I didn't want to fit in with them. I didn't even hang out with my own kicking team at Lucy Laney and they were black guys. What in the world would I have in common with these dudes? But I had no choice as they put my stuff in the back of the Explorer. The punter guy, Dorn, was driving and I prayed, "Alright, God, I know I was hanging out with some shady characters back home. I mean, I know my Damarius is a hothead, but I can't take this *Leave It to Beaver* crew."

"Perry, you want to ride in the front or the back?" Billy said to me.

Their kindness was making it hard for me.

"The back is cool. I'm a let y'all do your thing." I thought that by taking a backseat, it would not make the conversation be on me as much. However, I was wrong. We didn't even get through Atlanta without them asking me tons of questions. Was I excited about the season? Had I ever been to the beach before? What did they think, all black men never left the town they were born in? When they realized I was tired of the questions, they turned on some Christian music. The three of them started singing and grooving, and I felt like I was in the Twilight Zone. They were praising the same God I loved, but the way they were doing it was as if, for me, they were speaking Spanish.

"Is the music too loud, Perry?" A.J. asked from the front seat.

"Y'all do your thing, I'm going to take a nap," I replied as we drove down Highway 75 to Highway 17.

We were headed down to Savannah, Georgia, where my family had vacationed before. I was so happy we were almost there.

There was a big welcome barbeque for all those who were putting on the professional Christian camp; I was told they have the Week of Champions every summer. Professional athletes, former pros, and college players come to put on a camp for the island kids. Billy's dad was one of the organizers.

He said, "We're going to have to go right to the barbeque. I don't want to hear my mom's mouth about how we're late."

That was cool with me, because they hadn't even stopped for gas and we were on E when we got to the island. I was ready to chow down. But the barbeque didn't taste anything like Howard's back home. I hated to be rude but the stuff was bland. The guys offered me to sit with them; however, I felt more comfortable sitting by myself drinking a Coke. I looked around at the mostly white families and wondered why in heck did I come? Then a man said, "Excuse me, can my family and I sit here?"

I looked up and was happy to see another brown face. "Yeah, sure!" I said to the gentleman and his wife and three kids.

The man sat next to me and introduced himself as Coach Brown.

He said, "I'm head coach at Virginia State University, up in Etherege, Virginia. I heard you were going to be here; boy, wouldn't it have been great to have you on my team."

We shook hands but I looked a little bewildered. His wife saw my confusion and said, "Yeah, he knows you, hon. He studies football day and night."

"Yeah, I do know you. You're Perry Skky Jr. from Georgia, right?"

"Yes sir," I said.

"I used to coach for the University of Virginia; we've been trying to scout you since you were a sophomore, when it was your breakout year. Where'd you commit to?"

"I'll be going to Georgia Tech."

The coach then introduced his kids. "Clay, he's a quarterback in middle school right now, my daughter Carmen, and my youngest daughter Cassie."

"Hello," I said to them.

As soon as the Browns sat down, I felt more at ease. The conversation just flowed and I don't remember what we were talking about but it didn't seem forced. It was natural. I honestly felt that it was a black-and-white thing while we were eating in a club house that overlooked the beach and the view was spectacular. The blue waves running into the calm white sand looked to be calling my name. The Brown kids wanted to go out and have fun, and I felt a little sad. I didn't want them to leave me behind, but how could I ask to tag along? Mr. Brown looked back at me and told his wife, "Hun, why don't you go take the kids out. I want to talk to Perry for a minute. I'll be out in a second."

"Alright, sweetie. Perry, it was nice meeting you. I'm sure we'll see more of you this week."

"Yes, ma'am," I said.

"You want to walk out front with me, son, towards this neighborhood?"

I was still dozing off when Billy had driven into this exclusive country club. Walking a ways to see the three-million-dollar homes would be cool. As soon as we got outside, though, Coach Brown said, "Something's on your mind and don't tell me nothing. I coach ball players. Though I don't know you and you don't know me, you know I care, so? For real, what's up?"

"I don't know, coach, I just feel out of place here, that's all."

"I understand a lot of my boys that used to play with me at Virginia used to feel the same way, and quite frankly, that's why I get a lot of them to come to my HBCU. They don't want to mix up life just yet, but let me be real with you, son, the world you lived in in Augusta was pretty sheltered. I know you came into contact with white people."

"Yeah, I have, but to ride in a car with them, to stay in a room with them, to do everything with them and see nobody that I can identify with, I can handle it but I'm not comfortable."

"I'll be the first to admit," Coach Brown said, "they do have some different ways. White folks can be a trip. But in reality, let me school you real quick. I know your chaplain brings some good guys here to camp, and I know you're only here because you're trying to grow your relationship with God, true?"

"Yes, sir," I said. "True."

"It's okay to be proud of who you are—a strong black young brother who has got mad skills given to you by God, and you might come across a lot of crazy white people who are still bigots, but here at this camp and hopefully for the rest of your life, you'll start understanding you don't just need to be hooking up with people because of their skin color. In the end the only race that's going to matter is the one that's saved, and if you have to be partial to a color, black and white don't matter because you have the red blood of Jesus running through your soul. Son, in other words, what I'm saying to you is you need to get to a place where you're looking for the hearts of men not seeing any color."

~ 5 ~

Intersecting with Trouble

I was so very thankful that I bumped into Coach Brown at the welcome dinner at Hilton Head. With kid gloves, he let me know I was tripping; not that I shouldn't be uncomfortable in a different environment, but I didn't have to have the race card on my shoulders constantly. My life was about to change, and to soak up all that God had in store for me, I could not have hatred in my heart.

Ironically after all that "race" talk, as soon as we got back to see everyone, people started coming up to me finding out that I was going to Georgia Tech. I met all kinds of alumni, very excited about Perry, the athlete, and not Perry, the black guy, and of course, everyone else was white but it was cool—real cool.

When we got to the resort where we were staying, it was a place called Palmetto Dunes. It was an absolute maze—probably fifty different apartment places within this one community—but all of it had views of the beach or had access to it. And our apartment gave each one of us our own room. It was my first vacation without my parents and I was living large. Even though my method of partying was different from my roommates, I needed to make sure I didn't get into any trouble. They asked me if I wanted to go to the beach with them to work out.

"No, you guys go head," I said to Billy. "I'm a stretch a little bit first. My knee got tight with the drive. And then I'll catch up with you guys out there."

"It's getting dark so I hope you'll be able to find us."

"Oh, I'll just wear a white T-shirt. It'll be cool."

They tried to give me directions as to where they would run, because at night patrolmen didn't like you to be on the beach. It made sense since there were no lights out there or lifeguards on duty. However, you weren't banned from going, and you were just out there at your own risk, so I knew I'd be fine.

"You sure you don't want us to wait for you?" Billy asked me.

They had been overly nice asking me which room I wanted—the four of 'em were pretty much alike. Making sure that Billy's mom got the foods I liked to eat for breakfast, well, I was a growing man—I'd eat anything. Having me write down the types of movies I liked to see because they were going to pick some up from Blockbuster later on that night. Enough was enough, I was thinking to myself, but then I calmed down, remembering what Coach Brown had said: "Everybody is different." My boys that I'm used to hanging out with and still plan to from time to time, even though we would be going different ways, they didn't cater to me that much. A part of me was thinking maybe they wanted something from me, but I dismissed that, too, trying not to see the bad in everything. When I got out there on the beach, I couldn't find the three of them. I had taken a little longer to warm up, so I didn't know if they had gone to Blockbuster or what, and I was a little timid about stepping out into the sand. Seeing no one around, the rushing waves that I could clearly see earlier when it was daytime were calling me toward them. If I wanted to be closer to the Lord and see something so magnificent only He could create—I was certainly in the right spot. And as the moon glistened on the water from Heaven, I knew I wasn't alone out there and so I began jogging. I hadn't gone two miles when I saw figures wrestling around in the sand. I didn't know if those were my fellow Tech teammates doing push-ups or sit-ups of their own, so I got closer. When I came up on the object, I had to slow down. It wasn't three guys. It was only one person, and there weren't any push-ups going on. I heard howling or moaning like the person was in pain.

"Awh, see now, Perry, this is crazy," I thought to myself.

This was something like you see on *Law & Order* or something. CSI or 24, I mean once something looks shady, a brother is supposed to turn around and walk the other way. We often joked about horror movies among my friends that if that were a black person in that role, the first sight of trouble—they'd be up out of there, not sticking around to get killed. How did I know the person leaning over didn't have a gun ready to turn around and shoot me or something? Still looking, I stopped running and walked slowly backward, but then I heard the word that made me go forward again. That word was "Help!" I could then for the first time make out that the voice crying out for help was that of a female and she sounded young and in trouble. I couldn't go anywhere, I had to lend a hand. I rushed over to her and knelt down in the sand, turning the girl over she clutched her abdomen area. Though it was dark, I could see her mangled blond hair and ruined mascara running down her face with a dark black-and-blue eye and a bloody nose. Her clothes were also ripped off. At the sight of me she just started crying even more—uncontrollably.

"What do want me to do? Should I leave you alone? You're hurt. I need to go get help. I don't even have a cell phone out here."

"Leave, don't leave. Leave, don't leave, me," she said, barely understandable.

"Lord, I don't know what to do," I prayed. "I don't even know what's wrong with her." I mean, how badly had she been assaulted, and where in the world was the attacker? Did she know him, was he still around, was there more than one guy? I certainly needed clarity. I was about to stand up and pace, just trying to think about this whole thing. Should I move her? Did I need to run and go get help and come back? If I left her alone, could something worse happen to her? I had no idea what to do. But I couldn't get up, because she grabbed my hand and tugged me back down toward her and yelled again, "Leave, don't leave. Please don't!"

The next thing I knew I couldn't make out anything that she said because I was bum rushed by a guy who knocked me over and started beating me in the chest.

"This black guy was raping this girl," the guy said as he hit me.

I tried to take my leg and kick him off, but someone else held my leg down.

"You ain't going nowhere," a country white boy said.

Someone else got up by my head and kicked sand in my face. "Now, how does that feel? Brutalizing one of our own, we not gon' take that," the guy hitting me in my chest said as he struck me again. With sand in my mouth, my feet being held, and constant blows to my chest that hurt, I couldn't even tell those fools that I didn't even do nothing to her. I was there just to help. Pretty soon my former anger came rushing back to me, like the rushing waves that weren't too far away from my beaten body. Seeing the clouds and stars in the sky, I became numb to the abuse, but I realized if it didn't stop soon, I'd wake up somewhere up there.

I had to be dreaming. There was no way I could go from trying to rescue someone to being brutally attacked. I mean, this wasn't *Roots* time or anything like that; this was the twenty-first century. Why did the guys just have to assume that a black person was responsible for violence?

Seeing the clouds in the sky spin around and around my head made me think I was checking out of here. And if that was the case, at least I knew the Lord in my life wasn't so bad. I had a lot of status and I had never stepped foot in college. Not that popularity or notoriety is something that people strive for, but I wanted to be the best football player, student, and son I could possibly be.

I had made a lot of mistakes, but the Lord had blessed me in a lot of ways. Forgiving me and giving me grace put me back on top. It was for me to lose and maybe that was how He wanted my life to end. Maybe standing before my classmates giving our student talk at our baccalaureate was truly my crowning glory. My pastor kept telling me the Lord wanted us on earth not to score touchdowns, not even to make A's or tons of money, but to be fishermen and win souls for him. Now that I understood that, now that I had told others about it with a sincere heart, was that all there was for me?

Then I felt lighter, like all the weight from the three guys that were pounding me was gone. I just knew I was dead, but then I heard snaps and a man saying, "Wake up, son! Wake up."

"But Officer, he was the one that hurt that girl. We were just making sure he didn't get away with it!" one of the guys that attacked me said.

Then I was getting my faculties back. I was lighter because the three guys were taken off me by the cops. I could not open both of my eyes, but with my one good eye I could see that it was nighttime. A flashlight was in front of me and a cop was holding it.

"Come on, son, we need you to wake up."

As hard as I tried to open the other eye, it was like I was too weak. Finally I managed to pry it open some.

"He did it. We're telling you, he attacked this girl."

"I ain't nobody," I finally pried out of me.

"He's lying, Officer. He's lying," one guy said as he charged toward me, trying to kick me again before the officer grabbed him.

Then I heard another officer say, "Son, I'm Officer Barret. Let me try to help you up a little."

Though I was a football player and had gotten knocked down by linebackers and DBs quite often, my body was not made to be constantly pounded on. I had just gotten over goons working me over and now I come down to the beach to work out, try to help somebody, and I become the victim. But even in all this I guess it was a good thing, because it meant I wasn't ready to die. As I heard those guys arguing with the cops, I silently prayed, "Lord, thank you for allowing this not to be the end. The more and more I try and simplify my life, the more turmoil comes my way. I never doubted your love for me and I guess in the midst of this crazy situation, it's clear that you sent them to come, you know, well, you know before I was gone. You must have something great for me to do. You must not be through with me yet? But I got to tell you, I am so full of anger and rage right now—I don't know if you can fix that."

As soon as I finished my prayer, the blond-headed girl, who was in a blanket, came toward me pointing. I didn't know what her action was about.

Had she forgotten that I was the one who hadn't done anything harmful to her? Even though my lip felt funny and I could taste my own blood, I was going to have to find a way to speak up and set the record straight, but she surprised me by saying, "It wasn't him! The guy that attacked me wasn't him."

"Yes, it was, we saw him over here," one of the guys who beat me up insisted.

"I'm telling you it wasn't him," she said emphatically. "Officer, he came after my attacker had long gone. I was out here alone and afraid and he wanted to get help and I didn't want him to leave me. But before he could make out what I was saying, those guys came and misunderstood. He was leaning over me because he was trying to hear me. It wasn't him, Officer, it wasn't him."

Thankful that my arms weren't injured, I raised both up to the sky, like "Duh, I told you guys. I didn't have nothing to do with this." But then the cop tripped me out. He wasn't even sure that she was sure.

"Ma'am, we just want to be sure, so we can find out who did this to you."

"How do you know that it wasn't this gentleman right here? You could have been so out of it that you blacked out."

I mumbled, "Sir, ssshe said it wasn't me. Wwwhat else do you need to hear?"

He stuck his hand in my face. "Let the lady talk, sir. We're going to get to the bottom of this."

"I know my attacker. I was on a date, okay? He misunderstood my intentions. He goes to my school, and after he took what he wanted, he left me here and smacked me around because he said I made it difficult."

The girl fell to the sand and started weeping, and regardless of color, I really felt bad for her. She looked up at me and started swelling, "I'm sorry, I'm sorry. I couldn't speak up before, but it happened so quick, them coming over to you. I'm so sorry." And then she dropped her head back into the sand and a female officer came over to her and comforted her. When I tried to sit up and tell her it wasn't her fault, something in my abdomen area started hurting really bad. I knew my face was swollen, my lip was busted, and I couldn't open one of my eyes, but what was going on with my stomach and I certainly didn't need anything to be wrong with my legs.

"Son, stay down," the same officer said to me, who wouldn't let me get a word in edgewise a few moments ago. "You look brutally hurt, son. The ambulance is on its way. Relax. Officer Grabt, we need to book these guys," policeman Barret said to the other cop.

"But we didn't know, Officer. We thought that this was the guy that messed with her."

"We didn't know," one of the guys defended.

"But you didn't ask me neither!" I finally got up the strength and shouted as I stood up, enduring the pain but thankful that my legs were fine.

"But you were laying over here, we didn't know," another one of them said.

"Hey, man, I'm sorry. Please don't press charges against us."

I couldn't stand for long. My stomach was really hurting and my head was, too. I sank back down and Officer Barret helped me.

"What's going on here?" my three roommates came on the scene and asked.

"Perry, we've been looking all over for you, dude, on the beach," Billy said.

"You guys know this gentleman?" the officer asked the three white players wearing G.T. clothing. Like I couldn't know white people. I mean, I really didn't hang out with them until now, but why did he have to assume that it was that way?

"Yes, sir, we know him. He is our teammate. He's staying with us on the island. We're here for the Week of Champions sports camp."

"But you called him Perry?" Officer Barret said, "This is Perry Skky Jr., the kid from Augusta? The best wide receiver in the state that Tech snagged?"

"Yes sir," Billy said.

"And you're our kicker, right?"

"We're all a part of special team, but yeah, what's going on here?"

I thought to myself, "Yeah, let's get back to that! Don't now try to act like I'm somebody. You got talked into letting the guys who attacked me go, and now all of a sudden you want to defend me." I explained to my three friends what had happened, the ambulance came, and I was wheeled into it alongside the victim I came to help in the first place. Never ever knowing that I'd be headed to the hospital with her, knowing this, I'm sure I would have run far away from danger. And who could blame me?

A medic stood between the two of us as sirens went off and we were rushed to the hospital.

"Sir, it looks like you cracked a rib," the emergency worker said to me. "I'm going to clean up your face a little here from the cuts and bruises that you got."

The girl sat up from the gurney.

"Ma'am, you need to lie back down," the worker told her.

"No, I need to talk to this guy, please. I'm Anna Pond and again I'm sorry! I'm so sorry. You got caught up in all of this. You probably wish you would have left me out there, huh?"

"Naw, sometimes I just wish I had a different skin color. If I would have been a white guy and came up on the scene, saw you there all upset, I don't think they would have been so quick to judge that the person helping was the one attacking."

"I know what you mean," she said.

Now I was really confused—how did she know what I meant? She was a white girl; she probably had it all, a princess spoiled from the first day she was on earth. I had no reason to think differently. I just knew like most people said, "A brother ain't got a chance," and that rationale was true more times than that was false, but Anna went on to explain, "Sometimes I wish I wasn't a blond-haired white girl."

"What do you mean?" I said, holding my stomach.

"People just look at me and assume that I am ditsy and have no wits at all. And that every time I smile and turn my head and my hair flips, I am coming on to somebody. Yeah, I liked the guy at my school a lot, but I never gave him any signals that we'd go out and he could . . ."

"No, it's cool," I said as she stopped, finally understanding what she meant.

"It's not easy being a Hispanic either," the paramedic cut in to our conversation and revealed, "A lot of people get me mixed up with being a terrorist. And I'm not even an Arab."

Both Anna and I let out a little chuckle 'til the pain we both felt settled us down very quickly.

"But you can't stop being who you are because some people out there misunderstand you, and you can't stop helping other people just because there are some ignorant folks out there in the world," he said to both of us. "This night was terrible for both you guys, but it's already looking up—you both survived and, son, these injuries you are sustaining won't keep you off the football field this season and I'll be watching."

"You better be because when I run through a linebacker, I'll definitely be remembering tonight."

"I'm going to Tech!" Anna surprised me by saying. "I'm from Bluffton, a town not far from here. Maybe I'll see you around on campus, if I still go."

"What do you mean, 'If you still go'?" I said.

"I don't know what happened to me tonight. I just don't feel the same," she said, becoming emotional again.

"Didn't you hear a Skky was here?" I said, trying to encourage her when I was down myself. "You made it through for a reason. It's only going to get better from here."

We pulled up to the hospital and they took out Anna's gurney first. Before they pulled completely away, she said, "Wait, stop. Thanks again, okay, Perry? I was really scared."

I waved my hand at her and they rolled her away, then the paramedics came back and got me, and as they rolled me into the hospital, I looked up at the sky and thought, "Lord, I was scared, too." The chaplain, Coach Moss, was finally in town. Billy had called him and he was there as well as the organizers of the camp.

"Hey, partner," the chaplain said to me. "You looking rough. What's up? You used to be a ladies man," he teased. "You alright, though, man?" he said seriously.

"Yeah, I'm okay," I said. "I'm just tired of the games, that's all."

"I heard what happened. You want to talk about any of this?"

"What's there to say? A bunch of white guys saw me near a white girl crying, and they just assumed I was hurting her, then they hurt me. Am I really going to be okay?" I asked, knowing he would tell me the truth. "I was going to camp in a couple of weeks."

"They are going to take a look at you now."

"My folks," I thought.

"We've already taken care of them. We've arranged a flight for them to come down from Augusta. They should be here shortly. I feel so bad about this, Perry. You were down here in my care. Why were you on a beach by yourself, boy?"

"Trying to spend some alone time with God, you know? It was paradise at first, then it turned to sheer Hell."

He chuckled and said, "Man, I understand. You did do the right thing, you know, trying to help that girl."

"I don't know. I don't know if that was the right thing at all. I got all these bumps and bruises; I was beat up for no reason. I don't understand how that could be the right thing."

"Perry, Jesus was persecuted and He died on the cross for our sins, not because He deserved to be there, but had He not done it, we'd have no hope. And had you left that girl there, maybe those three guys . . . who knows? Or anybody else, you know?"

"Yeah, I feel you."

I was glad to finally be connecting with him; it made all this not seem worthless. I could never know what it felt like to have nails pierced through my hands or to carry a heavy cross while people were throwing stones at me and to die a suffocating death in the middle of a storm. But having this experience certainly was a parallel one that I would never forget and certainly make me appreciate the Lord even more for going through all that for me. I thought about Anna and hoped she was okay as I waited for the results from all the tests they were doing on me for precautionary reasons. I had to realize that I did deserve a pat on the back. Though ignoring her lying out there would have been easier and definitely a less intense choice, it clearly would have been the wrong one. Jesus didn't take the easy road and forget me; being my brother's keeper didn't just mean taking care of my boys or the people I cared about, but it meant stepping in to help any person in need. I was given some pain medicine, and when I woke up, I was so excited to see my mom and dad looking over at me, I could tell they were both worried sick.

So I said, "I'm okay."

"Oh, son!" she said as she rushed up to me and kissed my forehead.

"Boy, we send you down here to help some little children and you getting whooped up on by a bunch of crackers."

"Perry!" my mom said with an authoritative voice that she used when she was talking about the senior one.

"What, I'm just calling a spade a spade! We know the boy is going to be all right."

"I am?"

"Yeah, you didn't break a rib, you bruised it real bad. You got a deep cut over your left eye and you chipped a tooth."

"I didn't chip anything," I said, letting the anger well up in me again.

"Settle down, son," my dad said.

"Naw, Dad, I'm just saying. They were talking about arresting those guys then they weren't, then they were again. What's going on with them? I want the police in here right now so I can tell all that I remember while I can clearly understand everything that happened because I want them taken to jail. Not 'cause I'm some stupid football player, but because they were wrong, and if I let the crap go, they might do it to some other brother."

"Son, I hear you," my dad said as he sat on the side of my bed. "You did a real good thing here tonight after being stupid and going out by yourself in a new place when it's dark. Boy, I hope you don't do that when you go to Tech. You're big and bad and all that, but you ain't that big and bad, hello?"

"Yeah, yeah, I hear you," I said as I hit my head back on the pillow, then had to hold my hand to it because it hurt.

"I just want the police to handle it the way they are going to do it, son. You're about to go to school, you don't need to draw any attention to yourself, and I certainly don't want your name out there with some kind of race hate crime. It'd just make some people in this state stop and take sides, and when you stopped to help that girl tonight—"

My mom cut in and said, "That was from your heart! And although those boys were wrong, anger cannot dominate the best part of you. Let it go, son, okay, baby? Not for your dad, not for me, not even for those boys; you got to let it go for you."

"They got to live with what they did to you," my dad said. "Let the law and their conscience take care of that. No need for you to continue intersecting with trouble."

~ 6 ~

Revealing True Facts

Over the last year I had been assaulted three too many times. It wasn't that I never got over being cut by a high school teammate or that Jayboe and his crew scuffled me around a bit outside of the debutante ball, but I moved on with life. I put it out of my mind; it was the world I lived in. Not that I deserved any of those attacks, but I'd overcome them; until the beating down on the beach brought it all back.

A week had passed and I just couldn't get over what happened to me. Food didn't taste the same anymore. I was dragging in my workouts. Everything on TV reminded me of the incident. And although sleeping was the only thing left to do, even that area of my life wasn't working out, because I was having nightmares. As a last resort, I counted sheep—I remember my mom telling me that would work when I was about four, and it did then, but it wasn't working now.

One night I got up from my bed at 2 A.M. and headed over to my computer. I wasn't really looking for anything in particular so I just surfed the Net or maybe the Net was surfing me because I wasn't looking at what I was typing. Some sort of way I found a blog page about me; it was a page listing all my stats from all four years in high school. It gave details about schools, which school I was choosing to go to and my hobbies and interests. I didn't remember filling out the questionnaire but that didn't surprise me; my mom and dad had me well represented, and as good as my dad was at the dealership, if things didn't work out, he would be able to become an agent. Amazingly enough, there was space on there for people to go in and fill out information about me; whether they were looking forward to me coming to Tech or not and how they thought I'd do in the ACC. I was surprised to see all the favorable responses, then of course, I found the one negative one.

"This is the backwoods of Augusta. I doubt this player will live up to the hype. That's why they didn't even win the state title, they hadn't played anybody. Just because the big black . . ."

I couldn't even read any more on the screen. I turned the computer off and got my pillow and just pounded it. Rage was welling up inside me. Somewhere between my eighth and ninth punch and my three kicks to the headboard, I tired myself out and dozed off. When my phone rang at 6:58 A.M. I was startled and half out of my mind I answered it, "What, what you want a piece of me?"

"Perry, Perry!" my sister's familiar voice kept screaming over and over again.

I looked over at my clock to make sure it was really morning and all this wasn't just a dream. It said six fifty-nine.

"I'm glad I finally caught you," she said. I did not respond. "Brother, I know you're not okay. I left tons of messages for you. Every time I call Mom, she says you're out running so early in the morning or you're sleeping in the middle of the day. I'm so worried about you, Perry. Will you please talk to me?"

Well, when my alarm clock went off at seven, I jumped. It

was like the least little thing was disturbing me. Payton was right, though. I had started my day off so early and I hadn't returned any messages and I was dozing off at odd times because at night sleeping was more torment than pleasure.

"Perry, please open up to me. Please talk to me," she pleaded as I turned off the buzzer.

"Listen, I got to go run, we'll talk later. I'm fine, I'm cool. No need to worry about me."

"No, do not hang up the phone. Please do not do that. I've been praying for you. Please let's talk."

I couldn't just shut her out. My mom had told me too many times to call her.

"You don't have to go into any details. I know what happened—I know what those boys did to you. I just wanna make sure you're okay. I mean, when I moved up here to Georgia, white people were crazy. My suite mates, one in particular, didn't like me at all. She thought just being connected with a black person in any way was going to ruin her chances of getting into a sorority. When I went out to Velar's house, right before I even came to Georgia—Denver was a culture shock for me, too. You know Augusta, our area of town, it's all black people and I was comfortable in that environment. I went out to Arizona and it was some of everybody, which was great. I mean, I learned a lot and liked it, but it took me a while to not be apprehensive."

"Okay, so what's your point?" I just cut in and asked her.

"Well, I remember going into the grocery store and the man didn't even acknowledge me. I was standing there for the longest time saying 'Excuse me.' I took a number and everything, and he just went and helped a white person before me. I was so angry, so mad; I guess I'm just trying to say I understand if you're mad; if you want to go shoot all of them."

For the first time in a week, I chuckled. "So you had some feelings like that seriously or you just trying to make me feel better?" I asked.

"Seriously, I've been there but I can tell you as I kept the courage to stay at Georgia and gave white people a chance, I found out there were some crazy black folks running around there and some wonderful white people."

"So everybody's not bad, huh?"

"Everybody's not bad. But every time I gave my frustrations, my insecurities, the stuff that upset me to God, I could keep pressing on. And though I'm praying for you, brother, you got to pray for yourself. God is the only one who can take this yuckiness you're feeling and make it something wonderful."

"Yeah, that sounds good and I appreciate you calling, but look, sis, I'm just really not right there now. I'm not mad at the Lord or anything like that, but . . . I don't know. I just got to figure this out my way. Cool?"

I didn't mean to just hang up the phone on my sister but she would have kept talking forever, so I just leaned back in the bed after hanging the phone up and looked up at the ceiling. I was too bummed out to go run. I was still a little tired from staying up all night; I must have dozed off because I woke up to Damarius jumping on top of me.

"Hey, hey, hey?" I said, waking up and grabbing my bruised chest.

"Awh, man, I'm so sorry. For real I'm sorry. I forgot."

"D, man, you can't hurt him like that," Cole said to him.

"You must have turned off your ringer or something. You won't return any of our calls."

"Yeah, after I talked to my sister, I just needed some time, ummm, let's hook up later on."

"Boy, please, we ain't believing that," Damarius said.

"We asked your mom if it was okay for us to come over

and she said you were still in the bed and we were a little worried about you. So hey, we're here."

"I'm straight. Y'all don't need to worry about me."

"Perry, man, let me be real with you," Damarius said as he looked me square in the face. "When I was all down and out about Ciara's death, you would not let me wallow in it. What happened to you wasn't cool at all, and if I could go out and find those white boys now, I would punch their faces in."

"Like that's going to fix anything, knucklehead," Cole said as he plucked Damarius on the top of his head.

"I'm serious, while you were gone, man, Cole and I got stopped by the cops."

"For real?" I said, interested in what he wanted to tell me.

"Check this out: We were sitting in the grocery store parking lot when the po po's came up behind us, tag's current, showed him driving license and registration, and he gave us a hassle for no reason. He said we were supposed to be in the store—I mean, how did he know we weren't waiting on somebody."

"White dude?" I looked up at Cole.

"He telling the truth," my friend said.

"What, you don't believe me, racial stuff is out there, bro', we were on the wrong side of town. That's why you got to watch your back. Cole, you too when you go to Columbia and y'all need to make sure y'all keep yourselves healthy. How you recovering, Perry?"

"I'm doing better, because let me tell you, when y'all can't play ball anymore, school ain't gon' care about y'all."

I know they were supposed to be there to lift me up, but the truth they were telling me was only bringing me down more. Why should I think NCAA schools cared about me when my stats went down after I got hurt in the championship game? It had been a big argument about them playing players, schools getting millions of dollars off the football team, but all we get is a scholarship worth a few measly pennies. Naw, scholarships were worth more than that—going to Tech was roughly twenty grand a year. My sister and I had heard my friends; Payton had wanted me to remember both of them had valid points, but I had to find my own way through the truth that was troubling me, but could I do that before I broke down?

The next day I woke up to the smell of my mother throwing down in the kitchen. Being that my dad was spending so much time at the dealership trying to get things on the right track and I was doing my own thing, she really wasn't fixing big meals. As my nose followed the scent from my room to the kitchen, I was thankful that I had gotten a good night's sleep, but my time clock had been so off I had realized that it wasn't the next day. I had slept through the afternoon after Damarius and Cole headed out. It was just five o'clock. My dad was in the dining room helping my mom set the table. It was such an unusual sight that instead of going to see what she had brewing, I went and said, "Y'all getting out the good china? We must be having company. I'm headed back up to my room, I didn't mean to disturb y'all's plans."

"No, no, son, it's good to see you up," my dad said as he came over to me and gave me a big hug.

"Yes, we are. It's great to see you up. We didn't want to disturb you."

"Pat, that is not true. You checked on that boy about twenty times."

"Well, I didn't wake him, though."

"I'm all right, you guys," I said to my folks, not knowing myself if that was the truth.

"What's going in here?" I asked, wondering what the preparations was all about.

"Oh, just some other black dealers from around the South

came in town this morning and they're coming over tonight. We're having a big meeting."

"Everything straight with that?" I looked at him in a way that hopefully he would understand. I didn't want to lead on my mom that I knew things were shaky at the dealership front, but I certainly wanted an update. Last time we were together it was all about me and the ambush. I forgot to ask him what was going on in his world.

He whispered in my ear, "Why don't you go on up and get dressed and come back down for the meeting? It might be pretty informative for you to sit in on the meeting. I appreciate you asking what's going on, son. What's mine is yours, so you might as well learn all you can from some men who are actually facing similar problems with the manufacturer."

Though I still wasn't my old self, because I had come so close to death, I realized that I had wanted to care more, be a better son, really try and bond more with my dad. Months back, sitting around the table with a bunch of old men wouldn't have appealed to me at all, but now having lived through some gruesome things, in order to deal with them, I had to be mature. And in order for me to be more mature, I had to do more mature things.

My mom said, "Perry, don't you think it's going to be boring for this boy?"

Most people would find it odd that she referred to both of us by the same name, but it was just the way she called me, it was just the way she called my dad that we both knew the difference.

"Honey, I know what's good for this boy. He's been laying around this house all day."

"Naw, naw, naw. I don't want you guys to fight," I said to the two of them. "Mom, I want to be in here."

"Okay, that's fine."

An hour later I stood by my father at the front door and

we welcomed three interesting characters into our home. The first one through the door was Mr. Randall, from Orangeburg, South Carolina. "Wow, Skky, this is the blue collar football player, huh?"

"You mean blue chip?" my dad corrected his colleague.

"Yeah, we've been reading about you all the way up in South Carolina. Nice to meet you, son."

The short bald man who appeared to be in his late fifties headed straight over to my mom's spread. She cooked steaks, lamb chops, and grilled shrimp on the barbecue. Green bean casserole, mashed potatoes, and her homemade liver gravy with grilled mushrooms and onions all mixed up in it and her cornbread sweet rolls made it even hard for me to play host and not be over there with Mr. Randall grubbing down.

"Perry!" my dad said as he hit me in the side; I was looking at the food.

He said, "This is Mr. Brickhouse."

Mr. Brickhouse also appeared to be in his fifties, but he had all his hair and he wore glasses. He was from Chattanooga. He went in to say something to my mother. Then I looked at the last guy eye to eye. Like me, he was six foot three. It was Mr. Barksdale from Montgomery, Alabama.

"Son, I'm really proud of you. I got a son down at Alabama A&M in Huntsville and he only wished one of those big schools recruited him. He's doing good and working it out, but you got a great opportunity in front of you. Make the most of it now."

"Yes, sir," I said.

After we all ate dinner, the meeting started. If I had had sleeves on, I would have rolled them up to get ready to learn something, but it was summertime, and although my parents had on the AC and I didn't look like a slob for the occasion, I wasn't that dressed up. But I rolled up my sleeves in my mind; I seriously wanted to understand all their plights.

My dad took the lead and said, "So thanks, guys, for coming down. Let me just jump right in here and recap everything so we all hear the same information. I think I've been talking to each of you individually and we just decided to come together collectively and put all our cards on the table."

The gentlemen were nodding their heads, pulling out their pens and their paper. They, too, were ready to make a difference for their business, and to see older black men partner like a team was a good sight.

"You guys know that I inherited my dad's business?"

"Yes, Skky, I knew your father," Mr. Barksdale said. "I certainly miss him at our black dealer meetings."

"I appreciate that," my dad responded. "And my father built this business from nothing and it has been profitable for years and I am not here to downgrade his business savvy, but he's from the old school."

I had to admit it sounded funny coming from my dad like he was all hip and everything. Where did he think he was from? He definitely wasn't a New Jack City brother.

He continued, "But he never rocked the boat, he never questioned anything that came from the manufacturer. I mean, he was just happy they were financing his cars, and it wasn't until about five months ago that I was sending through applications for some of my black clients, and they were getting accepted but just with higher interest rates. And the folks were charging for the same credit score, the same income, the same amount of debt on a white couple, and it just happened too many times for it to be a coincidence. Never was it positive for the black customer, so I called it on them, and ever since then they've been squeezing me a little too hard, not accepting some of the black ones at all. So I've been looking at other means of financing. It just made it a lot tougher. When I started asking, some of you guys had similar issues. So now we're all here to think and figure out a solution."

The short man from Orangeburg said, "I could get a good deal in the market, Columbia, Charlotte, places like that. Though I'm down there in Orangeburg, they put me down where the white folks didn't want to go. I was able to come up with the two grand down payment, but they're only giving me six months' profit before they start eating into my start-up capital and I just felt like after I started talking to some white boys and their new businesses that I should get the twelve months to twenty-four months like them."

"Right on," Mr. Brickhouse said.

I couldn't say I understood all he said but I certainly heard him. Basically he was upset because they wouldn't give him a dealership in a prime location and they weren't giving him a lot of time to be successful, and if that were me, I'd be pissed.

Mr. Brickhouse began, "Now see I'm in a good market but there's trouble with that, too. I'm down in Chattanooga and my dealership has been open for sixty years but it was worth a million and they acting all crazy blue sky on me just to get the man a profit. So I had to pay two million for the place. Instead of them coming in to help me ask for the right price, they just wanted me to come up with four hundred grand anyway, so I had to take out two loans. Basically me and my family are living in a shack and I only have six months, too, to start making money. And of course, I have lost some of the loyal client base, because it's a new black owner. Word's spread real quick about that. It's like they want me to fail."

Again I wasn't familiar with the term "blue sky," but it looked like he had a great location, they made him pay double what the place was worth. Wow, that seemed so unfair. We all turned to Mr. Barksdale and he said, "Well, I couldn't qualify for two hundred grand with all the other things I got.

I was just telling your son about my son in college, and although he's got a scholarship, it's only partial and my daughter is just graduating from Howard. I got a deal with a partner. I had applied before him but it looked like they wanted him to apply for the deal so instead of cutting me out because they knew I'd sue, they made us partners. I had to come up with a hundred grand and he had to come up with a hundred grand. That's how we got to the ten percent down on the deal. But the problem is they act like he is the one who knows everything and I'm the one running the day-to-day stuff and it's just a lot of conflict; me getting forced into a partnership with someone that I didn't even know."

"See, this was just way too much," Mr. Randall said. "All of us have different issues but it is just clear that they are just trying to keep the black man out of business."

"I don't necessarily say they are trying to keep us out of business but they are certainly trying to make us not make as much money as there is to be made in this business," Mr. Barksdale said.

"Yeah, but if we can't make money, we're out of business," Mr. Brickhouse added. "Okay, so we're all here now trying to figure out what we're going to do."

Nobody asked me to say anything, I was only there just to listen, but with all I'd heard and all I'd been through, enough was enough. So I said, "Well, y'all got to do something."

"You think so, huh, young blood?" Mr. Barksdale said.

"Yes, sir, inequality can't be tolerated."

"But this is our livelihood," Mr. Brickhouse said.

"But if they're already controlling you by putting you in a tight situation, what are you going to do, continue to be squeezed until you have nothing or push back so that the pressure stops?"

I couldn't believe that I had put a smile on my dad's face. All four of the gentlemen nodded at me as if I had given them the go-ahead to go to war. I had only explained that I had to do what was right, but was that the best advice?

Every year the automobile manufacturer took the top dealerships across the country on vacations and gave them banquets, and awards to celebrate their accomplishments. This year my dad's place was being recognized for being the first African-American dealership that they had and paid tribute to my grandfather's memory and legacy. My grandmother, my mother, my dad, Payton, and I flew out to San Francisco for the big festivities. Just going from the airport to the actual hotel was a trip. All kinds of people were doing all kinds of things. Men were kissing men, women were naked, homeless people, tons of homeless people were trying anything to hustle up some money.

As we rode in the limo, my dad said, "Mom, cover your eyes!"

And she looked at her son and said, "Boy, please. This is better than what comes on my cable at home. You cover your eyes."

She was off the chain.

"You okay?" my sister asked as if I was an insolent myself.

"Girl, I'm fine."

I hadn't had a chance to talk to my dad anymore; my boys came back through that night and swept me out of the house. And I was actually excited that my chest didn't hurt as bad when we went out and played hoops. And although it had only been two days, he was so busy making sure that everything was taken care of while he was out of town that I didn't even see him until we got on the plane. And since our family was all around him, I wasn't able to say, "What's the plan, how are y'all gon' let those folks in charge know that y'all ain't having it?" But since he was never alone, I couldn't ask him until we got to the hotel.

"Pops, can I talk to you?"

"Son, I don't want you to worry about anything," he said to me. "Let's get everybody settled and we'll go for a walk later on, okay?"

"Yes, sir."

When we got to the penthouse suite, we walked into the quarters we'd be using for the next few days. We all marveled in the beauty. There was a room to the left that had a king-size bed and sitting area that my parents would be using and a room to the right with two double beds that my grandmother and Payton would be staying in. There was a pull-out coach in the center from the wall. It was so high-tech, the plasma TVs and surround sound and marbled countertops let me know that it wouldn't be too bad to be a baller one day so that I could have this kind of life. I had grown up not wanting anything but it wasn't every day that I flew across the country, rode in a big limousine, and stayed in a penthouse. It wasn't my first time being wined and dined being a top recruit—it had its privileges, for sure—but I wasn't used to this daily lifestyle. However, I knew just from the sight of it that I could get used to it very quickly.

Later that evening my father did keep his word. He and I went walking through Chinatown to Fisherman's Wharf to get some crab legs, or at least that was what I thought they were. We actually had whole crabs cooked in front of us on the street. The stuff was the bomb, and after we stuffed our faces, we walked along by the pier.

And he said, "Listen, you've been great. You've been real concerned about me and the dealership; you just really sparked something so I don't want you to worry about what I'm planning, what I'm going to do. I don't want you to worry about any of that. I just need you to worry about completely getting better. In a couple of days, son, you'll be headed into Tech. I need you focused on that, okay? Let your old man handle what's going on in Augusta."

"Yes, sir, I mean, just . . . but . . ."

"No, there ain't no buts, I mean nothing. You handle that and let me handle this. Cool?"

"Cool," I said, still tripping that my dad could be down with me.

The next day our family went to Alcatraz and my grandma must have been smoking something, but we all watched her. I don't know how she could have, but the way she was acting, it was just crazy.

She'd get in a jail cell and say, "Perry, come here, look at me. You think I'll be in jail like this if they catch me smoking one of my blunts."

"Grandma, stop," I told her.

"Boy, you know I'm just playing with you. Lighten up."

"Why are you so light all the time? Is it really the stuff you're on?" I asked her, just needing to know.

"Come here." She grabbed me into a headlock and we walked over to the cafeteria where the inmates used to eat on that eerie island.

"Ever since your grandpa left, there's been a hole in my heart. The Lord has been good—he's filled it—but I have been a little lonely and I just found myself again in my laughter. They didn't have female comedians back when I was your age, but I've been watching them Queens of Comedy, and I know I could have gave them hussies a run for their money back in the day."

"Grandma, you crazy. A comedian?"

"I'm just saying don't be so quick to think that I should be acting like I'm supposed to be in some old folks home. I want to enjoy the rest of my days—high, clean, drunk, sober, shoot, just seeing you do your thing makes me all proud like that. You know, I'm on cloud nine, boy. You love your grandma, don't you, sweetheart?"

"Yes, ma'am," I said.

"You think I'm a give you some money 'cause I know your butt ain't making none yet, but that's okay. I ain't going nowhere until you cash in. Then I'll come to you for the big house."

"Whatever I got, Grandma, it's yours, but I don't know 'bout all that."

"Come on, let's call it like it is. You know what I'm saying."

I was really digging her, because her and Payton weren't connecting at all. My sister wanted her to act more polished, and Granny was just being herself. Sometimes you just got to love folks for who they are and not try and change them. It was the night of the banquet and we were in the ballroom with several other families that were getting recognized for outstanding achievement. The night was going well. I devoured the breast of chicken, the salad, and the rice pilaf, asparagus, and rolls like it was nothing. My mother gave me the eye like, "Boy, you better slow down," and I looked back at her like, "I'm sorry, but it's gone." When it was time for our award and for them to recognize my grandfather, my dad hit my knee and said, "No worries, right?"

"No, sir."

He went up to the stage with a standing ovation. The president of the company said, "Perry Skky Sr. was a man of integrity. I remember years back when he came to our organization because he wanted a dealership. He didn't mind working hard, and because he showed us what a determined man could do, we now have launched a black dealer program to help other minorities realize their dreams of being in business as well. I know Perry is proud of what you've continued and what we're trying to achieve." Everyone clapped. "Here to accept this award is his son, Perry Skky Sr."

"Thank you. I don't know that I'd agree that my dad is proud right now with everything that we're doing." Whispers started going around in the ballroom. My mother got a really nervous look on her face. My dad continued, "My dad was willing to work harder to open the doors for others. He had to with my older brother, two sisters, mom and me, he had a family to feed. Thankfully, now there are thirty-two black dealers in this organization, and we've been talking and noticing that certain things need to change."

The gentleman who gave him the award leaned over and said something to him that none of us could hear. My dad tugged back on the mike and said, "In order for this corporation to continue to be successful, it must treat everyone equally, and because my father was a trailblazer, we plan to follow behind that steaming path and make sure we have just like we were a good ol' boy. You know what I mean?" A couple of people from the back were booing, but my dad said, "No need for that. I understand that this isn't the time or the place but my father can not only be proud that we get African-Americans in the business but he'd be proud when this company is truly intentional by helping black folks stay in business. Don't be mad, I hear the boos, but I'm just stating the facts."

~ 7 ~
Mixing It Up

When my father came off the stage of the awards banquet, surprisingly the boos were drowned out by cheers. I stood and looked around and saw white and black people in agreement that equality needed to be handed out across the board when it came to the manufacturers.

"Okay, okay. Can I just have everyone settle down?" Tom Hawkins, the president of the company, said to everyone.

When my dad reached the table, my mom said, "Okay, I'm ready to go now."

She grabbed her purse and motioned for Payton to get up.

"I'm not going anywhere," my dad said. "Sit down, Pat. We're staying here until the end."

She looked embarrassed and said to my dad seriously, "You might like people staring at you, but you just embarrassed us, Perry. I'm leaving."

He grabbed her hand and said, "Listen, I need your support here publicly even if you think privately I did the wrong thing. Okay?"

"Son," my grandmother said in a voice a few tables over could hear, "you know I am not ever a supporter of how Patricia feels, but I just can't believe you did that, using an award given in your father's name to push your own agenda. I'm really appalled and want to leave, too."

"Mom, we'll talk about this when we get into the room. You don't understand everything that's going on. All you ever saw was dad bringing home the checks. You never saw the other side to understand everything that he was going through to make that happen."

"Dad, it's like you're saying that Grandpa sold his soul to the devil or something to get this dealership up and running," my sister whispered, obviously not in agreement with my father either.

"Payton, baby, I'm not saying that at all. He did what he had to do to get his foot in the door, but I know my dad, and now it's time for me to do what I need to do to take everything to the next level. So, everybody just turn back around. Hush up, people are looking at us. It'll be over in a second."

A second seemed like fifteen long minutes, but thankfully after the event was over, my mom, grandma, and sister collectively went up to their room. I, however, stayed by my dad's side and I didn't say anything during the ceremony, but I appreciated a lot of what he did for himself and for others.

"Mr. Barksdale," I said, as he was the first to come over to our table.

"Skky, I'm really proud of you. You stuck your neck out there for all of us. It will make a difference."

The two of them shook hands.

"We'll talk next week because my family and I are headed out early tomorrow morning."

"Yeah, we are, too," Mr. Barksdale said. "Just know they got to make some changes now. You called them out publicly. I really, really appreciate it."

When Mr. Barksdale walked away, my dad came face to face with the president, Tom Hawkins. He pretended to shake my father's hand while smiling. However, I overheard him say,

"You just slit your own throat on that one, Perry. You didn't have to make a public spectacle about this situation, with everything your father has meant to our company. We would have honestly found a way to hear you out."

"No, I've been trying, Tom. You know I've been trying to get you to talk to me yet you keep pushing my concerns under the rug as if you can care less about what I think. Well, now whether you want to deal with it or not, you have to. You guys are treating the African-American dealers unfairly, and we're not going to stand for it anymore. Some of your white dealers also think that's wrong, so no threats scare me, Tom."

"Well, maybe that'll be your downfall. You think you've been treated unfairly, but you ain't seen nothing yet." And then he walked away.

If his words weren't rattling my dad, they definitely shook me, then I saw my father give me a fake grin as he swallowed hard. He was choked up. He was a little concerned that he had done the wrong thing. I think now maybe inside himself he wished he could take back his actions.

"Come on, Dad, let's go," I said to him as I pulled his chair back for him to walk out.

"Yeah," he said as he snapped back into reality, confirming once again that Mr. Hawkins's exit had got to him.

But before we could get out of there, a white dealer with an Oregon tag came up to my father and said, "Listen, sometimes it's hard to take a stand and make people realize what they're doing is wrong. What you did up there took guts, but I know for a fact that some of us get better deals than some of you guys and I don't think it is right. I talked to the company about it and they told me to mind my own business. You're doing the right thing."

As we walked to our hotel room, my dad made all this unnecessary small talk, asking if I liked the meal and did I appreciate hearing the great things about my grandfather and did I get to meet Mr. Barksdale's son, who also played football at A&M University.

"Dad, can we stop all the small talk?" I said finally, fed up with the fact that he was avoiding what we really needed to be talking about.

"What, what you mean, son?"

"Dad, what you did back there was pretty amazing, but a lot of people had a problem with it and I heard that Hawkins man, they might try and ruin you."

"They might," he said nonchalantly.

"Yeah, but you can't act like that doesn't bother you at all. I know you were a little ruffled after he talked to you; I saw your body language change. Dad, this is me. I mean, you want us to be close and all. You won't let me in on certain things and now that I am concerned you gon' shut me out. You shouldn't have to carry this alone."

"But that's just it, Perry. I don't know what I'm carrying, and though I want us to be close, boy, I'm still your dad and there are some things I do want to shelter you from. I exposed you to this because I wanted you to understand the inner workings of the corporate business. It's not all what it seems sometimes. A black still has it hard and you know that affects me, but a black man is also strong," he said as he placed his hand on my shoulder. "When things don't go as planned, there's a slogan you told me, 'Where midstream change, midstream adjust.' Crying over it or biting my nails over it isn't going to change whatever I'm about to face. Standing on my faith and being a leader and exercising my beliefs is what's going to let me sleep at night. God's got it."

I could only nod in agreement, whether or not he was ready for the backlash—he had to be as we entered the penthouse suit and my mother, my sister, and my grandmother started attacking him.

"Son, you know your dad would not approve of you embarrassing the company like that," his mother said to him before we even walked into the door.

"Honey, now, they're going to come after you. Don't think you could just recognize their wrongs and they're just going to sit back thinking that that's okay. You trying to stand up for all the black folks and now you're going to be the martyr; we can't afford that," my mom said, worrying about the financial repercussions of my father's actions.

My sister went over and gave my dad a glass of water that she'd poured. "I'm just worried about you, Dad. You are under a lot of stress. People were booing you in there."

My dad didn't know how to respond. Maybe he couldn't get a word in edgewise, because every time he tried to come at them with one thing, someone else came at him with something else. He sank on the couch and held his head. I didn't like my dad looking so disappointed. He'd just told me he had to handle it all, but being bombarded like that set him back some, I guess, and now it was time for me to step in and take off some of the pressure.

So I said to the three strongest women to our hearts, "Look, Granddad left the dealership to Dad because he believed he could handle it with character and integrity. I was able to sit in on the meeting, Mom. You know that when those other black dealers came over, I was appalled to learn some of their struggles. Martin Luther King once said, 'It's not what happens to me if I stop and help that man, but it's what happens to him if I don't stop.' Yeah, Mom, our dealership is doing fine."

I looked off to the side because that wasn't completely true, but I didn't want them to continue worrying since they were already ruffled. "But if Dad doesn't stand and help those who can't help themselves because they're new to the company and he sees things around him that he doesn't speak up about, he couldn't even live with himself then, but if we don't support him, particularly if he is right, and the world tries to tear him down, how can he stand up? I don't know." I walked over to the minibar and let them figure out the rest. My mom sat down beside my dad and gave him a kiss on the cheek. Payton went behind my dad and rubbed his shoulders and my grandmother called out, "Well, that's that. Perry, son, you can't let them think they gon' run over us. We'll be okay, we always have been; ain't nothing wrong with mixing things up."

Five days later we were back from our vacation and it was time for me to go to work. Though the fall semester wasn't here, Coach Red wanted the freshmen to take some classes so that we could settle into our routine both academically and athletically. I had no send-off at all, being that Damarius was in summer school and Cole had left the day before, headed to South Carolina to do the same thing, my sister was back at Georgia getting ready to train over the summer for cheerleading, and I had no girlfriend. My dad had taken the day off and I was going to follow him and my mom all the way to Atlanta, so thankful that on Tech's campus a freshman could have a car. My dad wasn't having it at first, but then my mom and grandma convinced him that I would be able to come home and to Conyers to check on them, which was just thirty minutes up the road. Knowing that I'd go home to get a cooked meal every chance I could, he went for it and I was able to have wheels.

I didn't really think I needed closure. I had waited for this moment for so long, but pulling out of my driveway for the last time, about to change residences, I was feeling something a little different. I'd been in that house for eleven years. It had represented security and empowerment for me and now I was leaving all that behind, about to make my own way and no longer ride on the coattails of my parents. And though I was following them to Tech, it was when they were about to head back that they'd be leaving me in the midst of downtown Atlanta, literally and figuratively. I'd be on my own, so I sighed and said to myself, "Am I ready for this?" A part of me was like "Yeah, man, bring it on," but another part loved the comfort of my old routine. Though I was starting to see that my sheltered world had protected me from so much, I knew that from now on, I was going to have to make wise decisions and protect myself. Plopping in a Gospel CD, I knew the only way for that to happen would be for God to lead and for me to follow.

My cell phone rang and I answered it. It was my dad. "So you ready for this? We're pulling on to campus. This is your new home, boy. My money can stop feeding you now. You quiet. What's up, Perry?"

"Yeah, I'm ready!" I said in a low-key manner, inwardly unsure of so much.

When we got parked near the registration office, my mom immediately got out of her car with my dad and came over to me and gave me a big hug. It was the middle of the afternoon and the sun was out shining so pretty across campus. Folks were busy going to and fro. I didn't care to pretend to get love like a baby from its mommy; at that point I needed it.

"Pat, let that boy go. We need to get him registered and get him in that dorm, put a little bit of food in his refrigerator, and get back up the road. You know I got to head to the dealership."

"You call me anytime you need anything, you hear?" she whispered in my ear as she gave me a kiss on the cheek.

"Yes, ma'am, Mom. I'll be all right."

"I know you will."

"Awh, I just can't believe my baby is going to college."

She wasn't the only one.

A lot of campuses had nontraditional setups for the athletes, and Tech was one of those schools. Not all of the football players would be in the same dorm; we actually were in
quads. My post was with three other freshman teammates. I
so hoped one of them wouldn't be Saxon Lee, but when I
saw him unpacking some of his things out of his dad's truck,
I knew it'd be only a matter of time before we found out
where each other was staying. My father and Mr. Lee exchanged pleasant welcomes, and as hard as I tried to hide it,
I looked around for Savoy.

"Man, my sister ain't here," Saxon said, calling me out.

"She's just coming down to train some this summer, but
I'm sure she won't be looking you up."

I made a motion like hey, that's cool.

"What room you in, Skky?" Saxon asked me.

"Two-ten."

"I'm in two-oh-nine. We must be right across the hall from
each other."

He just didn't know how relieved I was. Across the hall
would probably end up being too close, but I'd take that any
day over him being in my quarters. When I got up to my
space, none of my suite mates were there; I found a middle
area with two bedrooms on each side sharing a bathroom in
between both of those. The middle commons area had a 48
inch TV, a couch, and two chairs with end tables and a coffee
table. There was also a small kitchenette.

"Well, it looks like you get to choose your side," my mom
said.

But when I walked into one of the bedrooms, there was
stuff on the bed. I went into the other room and it was occu-
pied with suitcases, too. Then, I walked through the breeze-
way and saw two empty beds.

"Take your pick," my dad said.

"It don't matter," I told him.

As I chose the one farthest from the doorway, I told my parents they could go on and go, I'd be fine—I had a credit card with a limit on it and whatever I needed I could get, but my mom wasn't hearing it. She made sure they took me to the nearest Wal-Mart to load up on basics. When we came back, it was hard saying goodbye to them, but I knew it had to be done. Eighteen years of being under their authority had come and gone. I waved them off and headed back upstairs to my space. Before I went in, I heard voices from the inside. I knew someone was in there and I held my breath to find out who.

"Perry Skky," the familiar voice said as he opened the door.

I was surprised to see Lance Shadrach standing in our sharing space, but he didn't look that surprised to see me, like had he gone through my stuff or something; he reached out to try and give me five. What was that about me and white boys? Slapping hands was not my way of communicating. Before I could be disappointed about being thrown in a room with white guys, I saw a brother behind me. A little beefy dude that looked like he could hold his own. I had seen him before—he looked familiar—but I didn't know his name.

He walked over to me and shook my hand. "Hey, Perry." Shaking it the right way like he had some sense. "I'm Deuce Jones. I don't think we've ever been on a recruiting trip before together."

"Naw, man, I don't think we have either. You're a running back, though. You go to Lance's school?"

"I went to Lance's school, how 'bout it? We are freshman in college about to run the yard."

"A'ight, partner, I hear you."

Then another guy came out of my side of the suite. He was also white. I didn't have any problems with white dudes.

I just preferred to share my quarters with someone who understood my way of doing things.

"I'm Collin Ricks."

"Perry Skky," I said back.

"This is that good kicker from Alabama. He's here to take that job from the boy whose been missing 'em," Lance said as he sort of knew Collin, too.

I thought back to my summer at Hilton Head. It wasn't all bad. I mean, I did respect hanging out with the current kicking team, and although that was how football was up a notch, I knew it would be a dog fight seeing Collin and A.J. go after the starting job.

"Hey, Deuce man, my parents bought some food. You don't mind giving me a hand grabbing some of this stuff from my car?"

"Naw, man, you said 'food,' then I'm there. Yo', we'll be back," Deuce said to Lance.

"So, umm, when I came in, I noticed you and Lance had taken the other side. You know I know y'all from the same school. Y'all cool or you wanna switch over? Let them do what they do?"

"I'm straight either way. Is that better for you? Well, let me know we can get this straight. We can get to Collin before he even unpacks his stuff."

Deuce went over to Lance, and before you knew it, Lance was headed toward me all hot under the collar.

"So what's up, you want this to be a black-white thing?"

"Naw, man, it ain't like that."

"Well, I don't understand why you trying to get folks to switch over their room and all."

"I don't mind moving if Perry wants to share the restroom with Deuce."

"Nobody should have to move to make Perry comfortable," Lance pointed out.

"Handle it however you want to, I just made a suggestion, that's all. Take it however you want to take it. I'm going down here to get some food."

"Maybe we should get your own section in the refrigerator so you can mark your name on your stuff so we won't touch it."

I walked on out of the room so stuff wouldn't get out of control. Deuce followed behind me.

"Look, I'm a switch 'cause Lance and I, we tight. He does think he's a brother sometime. He's a weird white dude and he got an arm that's out of this world; you gon' love playing with him. I didn't mind rooming with him, but if I can get a little space between my old friend, that'll work great for me."

"Well, then why is he tripping?"

"I think you guys are a lot alike, plus he said something about he requested being in the room with you because his sister and your sister . . ."

"Yeah, they used to be roommates back at Georgia."

When we got down to the bottom of the parking deck where my car was, we overheard some guys saying, "Yeah, there goes those dumb jocks, they got a scholarship to come to Tech. It's not like they're going to be able to compete academically."

"See, Lance wonders why I got issues. I got to deal with this crap every day," I said.

"Yeah, Lance don't understand. He got too good of a heart. He doesn't realize that some people don't want us here or don't think we're good enough to be here," Deuce said, feeling me.

Deuce had come downstairs with no shirt on and some sorority girls were there whistling at us.

"Not everybody feels the way them boys did. Look at the hotties over there, wishing."

"You swing that way?" I insinuated about interracial relationships.

"As long as they ain't got what I got, I swing that way, part-ner, you know what I'm saying?"

"Naw, man, the sisters been holding it down for me."

"That's all I've ever tried, but I mean, I'm open to every-thing," Deuce joked. "I like you, Skky. I'm glad you suggested us changing up some things. Least we can be real with each other, partner."

The two of us slapped hands before picking up the gro-ceries. "I'm going to enjoy this year," I thought, "because Collin ain't the only one trying to take a starter's job and I'm here early trying to win the coaches over. It'll be a heck of a lot of fun mixing it up."

~ 8 ~

Convicting the Heart

When I woke the next morning for my first official day as a freshman at Georgia Tech, we all had to head to a meeting with Coach Red. But my nose was playing tricks on me—I could have sworn I smelled bacon and eggs and sausage in the kitchen. I knew I'd brought it, but I hadn't been up to cook it so why did I smell it? Peeking my head out my room, I saw Deuce in there whipping up some eggs.

"Man, what's up?"

"Awh, man, I hope you don't mind? I figured I would fix everybody something before we head to hear Coach."

"Naw, that's cool. Well, let me hop in the shower real quick," I said.

As I took a shower, I thought long and hard about what Deuce was doing. He wanted to make a meal for others and I had started off in the house with separation. I knew I was going to have to talk to Lance and Collin eventually to sort of smooth things over. I mean, it was no disrespect to them that I didn't want to share a bathroom with either one of them, listening to their type of music from that side of the house; I just wanted to be with my own. Maybe now I was rethinking if that was the right move.

"Good morning," I said with a bright attitude coming into the room with the three of them.

"Look who's in a good mood?" Lance said in a sly way.

"Awh, man, I know I was sort of rude yesterday. I didn't mean to be. Chalk it up to my first night being away from my parents?"

I held out my hand for him to give me dap. I wasn't really feeling no white boy trying to act black thing but it seemed like Lance liked playing that role a little bit. So to let him know that I was really trying to make amends, I conformed to his ways. Collin and Deuce put down their forks. I guess they were waiting to see what Lance would do—he slapped my hand. And a new era of peace in our house began.

"I'll buy dinner tonight," Collin said.

"What you mean, you don't have to do that. We'll be eating at the caf' soon."

"Yeah, but I think that's not going to start until tomorrow? I think the summer is only lunch and dinner is on your own. Something like that."

"Come on, you guys, we better hurry," I said, looking over at the clock.

We were supposed to meet Coach Red at 10 A.M. sharp, and it was nine fifteen.

"You're the only one who hasn't eaten, partner," Lance said, again in a slightly rude way.

It let me know we were cool, but we weren't really cool, which was cool with me.

"Alright, my bad, don't let me hold y'all up then."

"Naw, man, we gon' wait for you," Deuce said.

I grabbed some bread and put that sausage with the bacon and eggs in between, put it in a napkin, took a water out of the frig, and I was ready to go.

"Oh see, now who we waiting on?"

We all looked at Lance, who was tying his shoes. Walking

through the campus, the four of us looked around. Each of us were taking in different things, but it was a new experience leading us to greatness. I didn't want to fail on the path, and although I couldn't see the future, I was here and I had to go forward to experience it.

"Welcome, gentlemen," an older man with white hair and a bright smile said to the four of us. We went through the equipment room to the locker room, and though I'd been there before, it was real for the first time. It was no longer just a place I was deciding to come to; I was a "Jacket."

The older man turned around and said, "I'm Coach Bluff, been here at Tech for over twenty years, seen a lot of head coaches come and go, seen a lot of players show up and shine. We're glad to have you as our freshman class. It looks like one of the best recruiting classes in the nation and I know you boys won't let us down. Your lockers are dispersed by positions. Find your name up there; you don't have much time to get upstairs to the team meeting room, where Coach Red will address you."

"Sir, what's your position?" Collin asked him.

"I run the hive. Everything that goes on down here, I know about it. From the equipment room to the locker room to the training room to the med room and the rec room—I know about it."

It wasn't long before we were sitting in front of our head coach. There were eighteen of us present, and Saxon was even alert—not like at the battalion meetings, when sometimes he was asleep or didn't show at all. And who could blame him? It was now time to go to work. Our hearts were stirring. Looking down the aisles, I could see in the eyes of my freshman brothers that we were ready to get on the equipment, learn the new scheme, and beat any opponent. But then Coach Red started talking.

"So you heard from some of the other assistants. They got

your attention. They got you excited. They have you thinking that you can do anything, and that's why we wanted you here. Someday we do know you will achieve greatness. The question is, though, 'Were we right to believe in you? Do have what it takes to work extra hard to go the extra mile and not think about you but think about what's good for the team? If you feel you have what it takes, then I ask you a few questions. How many of you have had rifts with your suite-mates?"

I didn't raise my hand, but of course, Deuce hit me on the arm. Lance and I put up our hands.

"Ahh, Skky and Shadrach, did you both work it out?"

We both turned in, "Yes, sir."

"Good, because we are only as good as our weakest link. Do you guys think Virginia Tech is thinking about breaking each other apart? Or how they can come together so they can tear us apart when we play them this fall? I don't envy any of you. Some of you come here because the world says you're the best players and that might have been good for high school, but this is college level and now you have pressure. Well, some of you are walk-ons, want a chance to shine, but everyone says you are not worthy of being here. Then there are those of you that want a chance to start. This year you guys can knock some of my upperclassmen to the bench. Hmm mmm, well, in all those scenarios, it would take the courage of a lion to put aside the pain, to put aside the anger, to put aside the bad comments, to put aside all the prob-lems, to put aside whatever and focus on making that goal possible. Are you guys capable of making our team better?"

No one dared say a word.

"Well, I guess I better leave right now and send you all back home, take away your scholarships."

"Yeah, Coach, we ready, we ready," one guy shouted out.

"Thank you. Gentlemen, I need you to search deep inside

yourselves. You must really think about what you're going to have to sacrifice for the team. Put us first. Your parents, they'll be alright. School, we gon' get that done. That's a part of our success here. So I want you to understand what I'm saying here. Some of you guys have some bad habits that need to leave or we will not succeed this season. I believe you're winners; now you got to show me that you are. The academic advisor is about to be in here in a minute to give you guys instructions."

When Coach left the room, we all sat and thought. I knew I had some issues where race was concerned. I was going to need to get over some of the things that had happened to me so I could soar. It was challenging, but I didn't come here for a cake walk.

After our time with Coach Red and the academic advisors, we had a little lunch. All eighteen freshmen were chowing down, including me. The head trainer came to us and announced our physicals would be next before we could participate in summer workouts. We had to have our health cleared.

"Perry, son, it looks like you're getting taller," Coach Gibb said to me.

I was 6-foot-3½ or 6-4 in high school and now I was headed to 6-5. With all that going on, I didn't realize that my body was extending. I saw the cross around his neck and joked, "It must be all that praying to God I'm trying to do?"

"Well, son, that'll do it and that's gon' give you good favor out here. I got to admit even as a freshman, I ain't never seen a finer athlete come through here."

I got through my urine test, my eyes were clear, my bloodwork was normal, but he had concerns about my heart rate.

"Are you nervous about something, son? Just seems to be a bit abnormal. Take deep breaths."

"I still got a little pain in my leg. I was in an accident."

"Yeah, I have your record."

"You know about that?"

"Yeah, your parents let Coach know everything that happened. We don't want you to get back out there on that field until you're absolutely ready."

"But, I got to train. I'm fine. Are you really worried about my heart?"

"No, I just wanted you to be open and honest about what's going on with you. The only way my training staff can help you is when you let us know what's going on with you and emotional things play a part all the time. That's why we got the chaplain here full time, but you can't keep that stuff all bottled up inside, and I don't want you apprehensive about talking to us about anything, understood?"

"Yes, sir," I said.

When I got up and left the training area, I saw Saxon and Lance. I wasn't trying to eavesdrop on them but they looked all chummy, slapping hands and everything. I was actually going to walk right by, not like I didn't know them, but they were doing their thing and I didn't need to interrupt.

But then I heard Lance say, "Yeah and we can have the party at our place."

I stopped and said, "Hold up, what party are you having at our place? Who'd you talk with to clear that? You definitely didn't ask me."

"Oh, I should have known with you as their roommate we couldn't have no jam," Saxon said.

"Boy, you live right across the hall. Why can't y'all have it at your place? And even that would be too loud. I got kicked out of a hotel because of you. I ain't trying to get kicked out of my apartment. I just got here, you know?"

"Classes haven't started yet, Perry," Lance said. "We want to have a little party, meet a few of the little girls on campus, mix things up, enjoy life, and you not gonna tell me what I can and cannot do in my place."

"You not gonna push a party on me in my place, so I think we got a problem," I said, stepping up in his face.

"No such thing, we don't want the party to be dead anyway. We'll just have it at my place this time, Lance, it's cool." Saxon grabbed Lance's arm and walked away.

Later that night Collin, Deuce, and I went out to catch a movie. Lance said he had other plans. I didn't know if his party was tonight or whatever. It didn't matter. I didn't care. But when we came in, we were surprised to see our place trashed—bags of chips, soda cans, and beer bottles were lying all over the living room. Lance was on the couch with two different girls on both sides of him. The girls looked like cute sorority freshmen. If their hair hadn't been mangled all over their heads, they probably would have been classified as adorable, but to me, they looked like wasted fools.

Collin, on the other hand, said, "Dang, Lance, why didn't you tell me you were going to be entertaining some friends. Two seems to be too much for you to handle, guy."

"Oh no, I don't need any help with these two," Lance said as he kissed one on the lips right in front of us.

Deuce said, "Man, take that to the bedroom. Ain't nobody trying to see that."

"We want the living room," Lance said as his words slurred. "You guys go somewhere else."

"Come on, Lance, you not gonna let me meet the ladies?" Collin asked.

"Not these two," Lance said as he kissed the other one.

I had no idea what they'd been doing while we were gone and didn't even want to try and find out.

I bent down and told Lance, "Look, you are not the only one who lives here, and I don't appreciate you using all of my groceries to entertain your friends."

"Oh, oh. You brought this stuff?" one of the girls said. "Then let me thank you for it."

"No, don't you get over there and go to him. *Please*. We're sharing this house. He shouldn't have put it in here if he just wanted it for him. He told us we all could have some stuff."

"You know what, Lance? I don't even know why I waste my time on you, boy."

"You know what, Perry? Saxon's right. You think the world revolves around you. Don't be upset because I'm entertaining two cute ladies in the house and you have nobody. I heard his sister dumped you."

I grabbed his collar and wanted to choke him. He knew nothing of my relationship with Savoy. He didn't even need to speak of it as if he had all the specifics, and I could figure out that he was no psychiatrist. If he'd had any skills in that department, his own life wouldn't have been messed up. Here he was up in college trying to get ahead, and all he was doing was taking stupid steps backward.

"Y'all might want to put y'all shirts on," Deuce said as Collin just stared.

"Leave him alone," Deuce said to me. "Let him entertain."

"You better listen to him," Lance taunted.

"Whatever, Lance. You can't hurt me."

And he gave me a smirk like "Yes I can, yes I will, wait and see." But what could I do about that, but believe he was bluffing?

Somehow we got through the week without seeing each other, and the next time I saw him, it was Saturday afternoon. I was coming outside of my place to go to the track and run, but people were all in the hallway—Saxon, Lance, and some girl.

"Excuse me, y'all," I said.

When the two of them moved away, I was surprised to see Savoy standing by her brother.

"Hey!" I said, ignoring them two.

"Hi."

"You up here for good now?"

"No, just up here with my parents to check on knuckle-head."

"You know they got to check on me, but I got my friend here who's going to show her around today."

"Yeah, I'm a be your escort," Lance said. "We're going on a date."

"Yeah, you know my sister prefers Jerry," Saxon said.

"Sax, he's just showing me the campus. It's not that big a deal."

"Oh well, he's going to treat you special."

"Yeah, I'm going to be a gentleman. You do think I'm cute, right?" Lance asked Savoy.

"You're adorable."

I couldn't believe it. They were flirting right in front of me.

"Wait, Savoy, come here, come here for a sec." I grabbed her arm and pulled her through the two of them, over to the other side of my door. "You don't need to go out with him."

"What do you mean, I don't need to go out with him, Perry?"

"I mean, don't be talking about he's cute and all that. I can show you around today. I mean, I was just gon' run and that sort of thing, but I don't mind hanging out with you."

"I don't want you to have to go out of your way for me. That's why I didn't even bother to let you know I was up here, and I don't want you to seem like you're all concerned. If you wanted to hang out and be with me and stuff, things would have been different. You would have done things differently. I mean, I don't want these idle words to be because you see me talking to some other guy."

"It's not just some other guy. I room with him."

"What, what are you over there saying bad about me, Skky?" Lance said as I saw them share a giggle, but this wasn't funny. He couldn't hurt me, but him playing with Savoy and Saxon allowing that because he didn't like me was getting to me in a way that I couldn't explain. Yeah, I had messed up, yeah, I had done things to hurt Savoy, but I didn't want her to get in harm's way, and when she said it was great seeing me and walked away from me and took Lance's arm and he smiled coyly at me as they walked out of my view, I was crushed.

"What goes around comes around, hey, ol' boy?" Saxon said, adding insult to injury.

Instead of going to run, I opened my apartment and went back into my room and lay on the bed. It wasn't over; my heart couldn't let it be.

I didn't get a chance to sulk long. I mean, who could I be kidding? Who could I be mad at long? I was a player in my time. Lance and Saxon had their issues with me and they knew a button to push that would get under my skin; I just had to be stronger. Either Savoy and I would get back together, or she would make her own bad choices. I had made mine and I had to live with them. Who was I to prevent her from her own growing pitfalls? But before I could give more thought, my cell rang. I looked at the number and just laughed.

"Damarius, what's up, boy? What you been up to?"

"Uh, Perry man, I'm just trying to stay out of trouble, man, umm. Look, what you up to this weekend?"

"Man, got my new place down here and got some studying to do already. Just been in class a few days. Got some English and math to go over."

"Awh, man, please. Studying, man, you don't need to do

that," Damarius said. "You probably already know all the stuff they teaching even at Tech. It's not like you at Harvard or Yale or something."

"Boy, Tech ain't no joke."

"Naw, naw. I'm just playing, but look, umm, you know, umm, if you not busy . . ."

"Just ask him," someone in the background said.

"What's up, D? Who you with?" I questioned, sitting up on the bed, jokes gone.

"Nothing, man. I was just wondering, umm, if you needed some company and stuff? I got myself into a little trouble and need to hang out."

I didn't even need to ask if Damarius was with Jayboe. I was so sick and tired of that no-good lazy thug wanting everybody to be going nowhere just like he was.

"Ask him, D, now, ask him?" he asked again.

Then I questioned, "Jayboe with you?"

"Uh, umm." Damarius hesitated to answer my question.

"Hey, D, just say yes or no. He don't know what I'm asking you."

"Yeah."

"Man, why you hanging out with him?"

"Come on now, Perry, man, you wouldn't understand. You got it going on now in college and stuff. You left this world. I'm just asking can we come your way and hang low; we got a little heat on us. You know what I'm saying?"

"Tell him, we can be there in two hours."

"We outside of Augusta now, we can be there—"

"I heard him," I cut Damarius off. "I heard him."

I would do anything for my friend, probably because I was in a place in my life where I kept putting myself before him, though I was not responsible for Damarius not taking care of his grades and not hanging with the right people. Maybe me being selfish was a part of what got him in some of his own rut, but it wasn't just about me now; I couldn't bring him into my space now. Because just like I didn't want Lance to have a party because it wasn't just his, I had three other roommates.

"No telling what they been doing," I said. "I'm sorry, man, but this ain't just me who stays here."

"Man, see, I knew you were going to punk out like that on me. I knew you were going to think you were too good to help. Forget that I even came to you."

"Alright, if it's like that?"

"It's like that."

And then the line went dead. A few hours later I was running out on the field. It was a hot July in Georgia. I looked up at the sky as I took a break from running around the track and said, "Lord, I just don't understand why this stuff is so hard. When I try to do right, folks think I'm trying to be too good, but when I look the other way, I feel I'm letting you down. It's like no way to win; can you help a brother, please?'

"Skky, come here." I didn't even know Coach Red was out there watching me run.

"Hey, Coach," I said to him.

"You're really practicing, trying to get back into shape, huh? I don't want you overdoing it here. It's the middle of the day."

"Yes, sir, Coach. I just needed to clear my head."

"That's what I hear—you got a lot on your mind. The chaplain and I talked."

I made a mental note that whatever I said to one of the coaches wasn't safe and secure, not that no one could keep a secret or that what I said was confidential, but it was just good to know that conversations were not off the record here. Coach could sense that I was a little disturbed about him talking to Griff about me.

"No, it's good. I was going to talk to you this morning when I gave the talk to the freshmen. It's no secret, you're our prized catch—we're expecting big things. And that's a lot for anybody to handle. You're just a human, even though your ability is supernatural. You've got to be aware that some of your teammates are going to be a little envious of this. First of all, they're not going to believe the hype, but when they see you, they're going to be blown away. When they see you in action, they're going to be hushed up. When the upperclassmen come in here and you bring more buzz to this campus than we've had in a long time, some of them are going to be jealous. But what you need to remember is that in order to succeed, you must make this team succeed. You can't put up with nonsense. What I'm saying is we need to find a way to bridge all of this madness together and I know you can do it."

And then he just ups and walks away. I ran a couple more times and was relieved that my body felt good responding, but I kept Coach Red's words in my head. Maybe I didn't need to be such a hothead. Maybe if I put myself in my team-mates' shoes—even Saxon's and Lance's—it would allow me to see their utter disregard for me and understand it. Saxon was supposedly the best inside Carolina, but in every poll where they measured us two together, I clearly was the standout. Lance was an awesome quarterback, but he still wasn't getting as much attention as I was from the press. I never asked for any of it, but I saw how it could make some-one wanting the attention and not getting it a little uneasy.

"Man, aren't you from Augusta?" Deuce said as I came back into my apartment drenched in sweat.

"Yeah, man, what's up?"

"There's a car chase going through the city." He pointed to the scene on the TV.

"What?" I said, not even concerned about my wetness.

"Your phone has been ringing like crazy, too."

I checked my phone and I had multiple messages from Cole and my mom and dad.

I dialed Cole and said, "What's up?"

"Man, it's D. He and Jayboe getting chased by the cops. It's on TV and stuff here."

"Yeah, it's on here in Atlanta, too," I said. "What happened?"

"I don't know. Word is Jayboe robbed some convenience store. Damarius is just mixed in with him. I told that fool I was coming home," Cole said.

"He asked me if he could come up here for the weekend and I said no. I'm glad I did. The police would have been all at my door."

"He asked to hang low at your place and you told him 'no' with him running from the cops with nowhere to go? Dang, Perry."

"Was I just supposed to let him come through here?"

"I don't know, man, but look . . ."

We both held our breath and watched the TV as the car that held Damarius and Jayboe ran off the embankment.

"Man, if our partner is dead, then how you gon' feel then?" Cole said to me before he hung up the phone.

I couldn't say anything. I just dropped to my knees. I had to think heavily on what I was doing. The whole scenario was convicting my heart.

~ 9 ~

Restoring What Matters

With my left hand I grabbed my throat, unable to breathe at the sight of what the TV showed. J. Boog's car had gone off the side of the road and even the TV announcer could not speak.

Deuce said, "Is that your partner, man? Is that your friend?"

"That's my boy. He's just messed up with the wrong dude. Come on, Damarius, you got to be alright. Lord, please."

I looked over at Deuce and he was silently praying as well. We had never talked about our beliefs so I didn't know that he was into God and stuff.

"There is some movement," the announcer said. There must have been ten police officers with their guns drawn walking slowly toward the car. "Yes, we're confirming movement on the passenger side."

My phone rang and I answered it. "Hello?"

"Hey, man, I'm sorry I hung up."

"Naw, man, you right. I should have let Jayboe and Damarius come here."

"Naw, boy, that would have been crazy. Then you would have been locked up in this foolishness, too."

"Is he alright, though, man?"

"It looks like he's moving."

"They got him out," Deuce said to me as he hit me on the arm.

"Cole, you see that?"

"Yeah, man, he's alright."

Neither Cole nor I cared about Jayboe. I'm not saying we wanted him injured but let's just say we were definitely happy that our friend was okay.

"So what's going to happen to him now?"

"I don't know. You see them taking him into custody," I said to Cole as we watched the events unfold on TV. Couldn't believe my boy was getting arrested for robbery.

"I repeat, both suspects are being taken into custody. No one was injured in this twenty-minute high-speed chase," the newscaster reported.

"Dang, they ain't have to take him down like that!" Deuce said as we watched Damarius get tackled to the ground by four officers.

"Why does it take all of that, Cole, you know I mean? Brother already got it hard."

"They ran, man."

"They not even armed."

"I know but they're considered dangerous. You just got to pray for your boy."

"Yeah, I've been doing that. Look, you just take care of yourself up there in South Carolina."

"I'm in Augusta now. I'm gonna go back later on tomorrow but I'm at home for the weekend. Maybe I'll get a chance to see Damarius."

"You gon' go to the jail?"

"If I can! I don't know—maybe I might try and get him out."

"Alright, well, call me if you need some money or something."

"Cool."

We hung up.

"I just can't believe this!" Deuce stood in my doorway and said. "So your friend that was on TV went to high school with you?"

"Yeah, he was a defensive player. He was running with the wrong crowd. Really great at basketball but bad grades."

"I got some partners like that," Deuce said. "So what, you now gon' lay around and feel all bad and everything?"

"Of course I'm a feel bad. He asked me if he could come up here and I knew he was with that loser and I didn't want him to bring trouble to us. I mean, you know, I got room-mates and stuff."

"Man, you can take care of your friends and not worry about me."

"Yeah, and we get kicked out of Tech before we even get going good."

"I see what you mean. You did what you thought was right. We all make our own choices; we got to live with that stuff. Your boy is headed to jail. Maybe that's what gets him to turn his life around, you know?"

"What's going on in here, somebody die?" Lance came into the room and said.

With all that had gone down, I didn't feel like having a showdown with him, but I did want to know where Savoy was, so I asked.

"She's with her parents; she'll be back in a few. But we're about to have a party so don't even think you can have a dance."

"What you mean? She's your date?" I asked as I stepped up to the doorway. "You don't even like her. Just yesterday you had your tongue down two girls' mouths."

"So, I'm trying out a little bit of everything; vanilla, choco-late. Don't hate!"

"When you have bad intentions, I can't do anything but hate."

"Look, Skky, I don't want to have any issues with you. She told me all about how you guys use to be boyfriend-girlfriend."

"Wait, Shadrach, you dating his girl?" Deuce said with a little humor in his voice.

"Oh, don't think it's funny," I commented.

"Yeah, he gon' tell me what to hit and what not to hit, that's not his anymore. You better school him, Deuce."

"Take your friend and go somewhere else," I said to Deuce, "and thanks for, umm, you know, my friend."

The male bonding thing was a little hard for me. Deuce didn't even know Damarius and had already prayed for him and that had meant a lot. But Lance had ticked me off, and all I could do was slam the door on both of them. I needed my space. I needed to have some alone time with God. That was going to get me back on track mentally. I couldn't let Shadrach get under my skin nor could I beat myself up over the fact that I wasn't going to be a part of Damarius's stupidity, and even though I wanted to protect Savoy with every ounce of my being, I couldn't control other people. But I desperately needed the Lord to control me. So I opened up the word and started to read John: 1. Sometime later I fell asleep and woke up to loud blaring music happening across the hallway. When I came out of my room, Deuce was on the couch.

"You gonna get dressed, we gon' go over or what?" he asked.

I knew Savoy was over there and a bunch of other new cool hot girls.

"Yeah, give me a minute. Let me shower up and be ready to head out."

Before we left, though, I called Cole once more. He gave me the update that Jayboe had his people bail Damarius out.

The party was just a few feet away, but we couldn't even

get there quickly. The hall was lined with people and Saxon's place was crowded as well.

"Yo boy know how to throw a party," Deuce teased me.

"Yeah right. Saxon and I are hardly boys."

The music was killing me and it wasn't the beat or the volume; it was the words. It was like they'd gone and got the basement triple X-rated version of every song, and their living room–turned–dance floor was filled with honeys backing their thangs up as the music degraded them. It was a trip, and then I saw Savoy, gorgeous as I don't know what, wearing a cute tight black dress with her pretty light brown skin glistening as if she were shining more radiant than a diamond. She was smiling at Lance. I noticed two other girls upset that he wasn't talking to them. I was getting my looks, too, and that was cool. But I wanted the two of us to just be alone and to let whatever happens happen, but was that the right thought?

"Hey, Deuce, I'm a check you later. I got to get out of here."

"Wait up, man. I need to go, too."

"Naw naw, man. I don't want to take you from the party."

Next thing I know we were walking the campus.

"Why'd you leave the party back there?" I said to him after we had a few moments of nothingness.

"Man, I've been trying to go on my Christian walk ever since me and my girl had a kid and then lost it. I just felt the need to grow closer with God. I'm not all the way there, I feel contempt too easily—all them girls in there with no clothes on. Man, shoot, I been done slid so fast, that's why I needed to come out here in the air and just talk to the Lord, you know?"

"Yeah, I know. That's why I needed to come out here, get a little time. Maybe the two of us can keep each other accountable this year?"

"I'd like that, Perry, for real. I'm just finding out that that's the only thing that counts."

"I think you're right, partner."

We slapped hands.

As Deuce and I walked back to our apartment, it was exciting that not only had the Lord given me a teammate with great ability close to mine, but he'd sent me a new believer who wanted to please God just I did. That to me was a special blessing.

I hadn't had but a few good friends in my life, and one was Damarius, who was completely opposite of me. I always leaned towards what was right and Damarius always leaned toward what was wrong. I could only hope as Deuce had eluded that his bout in jail had changed that mind-set.

Then there was Cole. Physically he wasn't considered a ladies man but he had a girl who loved him to pieces. He wasn't considered overly handsome, and though he believed in God, he thought he was too young to pick up his cross and sin no more.

My only other pal was Jordan. We had the smarts thing in common and we didn't hang out that much. But to find a friend like Deuce, whose physique could catch the ladies and who was a stud in his position when it came to playing ball, and who was also smart enough to get into Tech and who loved the Lord, well, I felt lucky.

"It's amazing how much we have in common, huh?" Deuce said, almost reading my thoughts. Skirting my eyes, I stared at him. "What, did I say something wrong?" he asked.

"I just can't believe I was thinking the same thing."

"That's a good thing, right? We just said we gonna hold each other to the grindstone when it comes to trying to do all this God's way, but it seems like you have a lot on your mind, Perry. You want to talk? What's up? Tell me about this Savoy girl Lance has got you all rattled about."

"Okay, see, I wasn't trying to talk about that," I told him. Since Damarius and Cole were players, I never really talked to them about my love life. They always thought I wasn't sowing my oats wild enough, but it seemed Deuce really cared. "Awh, man, it ain't nothing. I can handle it."

"Come on, partner, it's obviously something. If you don't want to talk about it, I understand, but you must admit you really got a thing for that girl."

Maybe because I was trying to gain a sense of who I was, God knew that I needed a partner here on earth to keep me grounded. Keep me honest with myself to open up some so I wouldn't have to keep things all bottled up inside. Why not tell Deuce a little? The only way to know if he was a good friend was to share personal information with him and see what he did with it.

"She was my girl. My sister and her first cousin date. Trust me when I say I hate the fact that her brother is Saxon Lee. I can understand him. He seems a trip but what he shows you believe it, but Damarius, my friend who was in that car chase . . ."

"Yeah, the one we saw earlier today."

"Yeah, his girl died in a car accident and my girl was in the car."

"Who, Savoy?"

"No, my other girl."

"Dang, boy, you worse than a soap opera."

"Ha ha ha. I see you got jokes."

"Naw, I'm serious. Go head, go head."

"It just got me and my old girl close, and I went too far and messed things with Savoy."

"You cheated on her."

"Yeah, basically I guess I cheated on her."

"You care about the ol' girl?"

"I don't know. It was just all mixed up. We saw somebody die, you know. It just was a lot."

"So then when she found out, she broke up with you?"

"Yeah."

"And now you want her back?"

"I don't know."

"Well, until you know, don't you think you need to leave her alone?"

"I can do way better than Lance. Don't you remember we just caught him with some chicks the other night?"

"What is he gon' do with Savoy? I don't know, maybe she calm down his white behind."

"Maybe you're right, Deuce, maybe you're right. Until I know what I want, I need to leave her alone."

"Sometime the only way you can find out what you want is to try some other fish in the sea."

"I'm just not feeling the other girls who are trying to get with me, because they think I can ball. I don't know, maybe I'm a little past that, been through a bunch of stuff. Somebody I can talk to, somebody who doesn't care if I score a football or not, you know."

"Yeah, that's how I feel about my girlfriend at home, but you know I'm in college and I do want to try a few other things. Man, we too young to settle down, right?"

"Right," I told him.

We had agreed we'd stop through the party and grab some food so we could head in for church tomorrow morning. However, when I saw Savoy's lips kiss Lance's, I was madder than a wild lion needing to be caged.

"A'ight, partner, hold up, hold up," Deuce said, stepping in front of my way.

"Man, move back. That's not cool. She don't even know what she getting herself into."

"Her brother is here. She won't be getting into too much."

"Saxon is probably too drunk to even notice what is going on."

"Come on, Perry, let's just get some food and go to the room like we said we were."

"Naw, man. I can't do that. Get out my way, dude, seriously."

I had to go talk to Savoy. I had to let her know that she was looking like a tramp in front of all the football players. Her brother may have been locked in his bedroom getting busy with some girls he didn't even know. But let's face it, the MO was different for females. They couldn't do like we do. I went over to Lance and swung him off Savoy.

"What are you doing, Perry?" she asked.

"We need to talk."

Before I could grab her hand, I was pushed from the side.

"What, you want to fight me, Perry?" Lance said.

"I told you to leave her alone and you didn't leave her alone. If that's what it takes for you to hear me—let's go," I said to him.

"No, Lance, there's not going to be anything like that. Perry, come on," Savoy said to me as we left the party. I grabbed my key and opened the door to my own apartment.

"Come on. We can talk in my room."

Before I could shut the door, though, Lance came in behind us. Now we had gone from a big crowd to just the three of us.

"You don't want me to kiss her, but you gon' bring her into our apartment," he said.

"It's none of your business what I'm doing," I told him.

"Lance, please, please give us some time to talk. I got to talk to Perry. He's tripping."

"Yeah, but he can't come up in my face and push me like that, Savoy. That's much disrespect, and I'm not gonna take it."

"Well, you not gon' kick me out of my place either. I live here just like you."

"Fine, we're going to my room," Lance said, grabbing Savoy's arm.

"Lance, please, please, just let me talk to him," she pleaded, moving away from him.

"You don't have to beg that boy," I said as I walked her toward my room.

"So what's going on?" she asked me when it was just the two of us alone standing there in my bedroom. "I don't have much time. I got to meet my parents in a second."

"Why, Savoy?"

"Why what, Perry? I don't owe you any explanation. You owe me one. I'm with a guy and you break us up in the middle of it like I've committed some sin. We have no commitment; remember you're the one who broke it. It's over, there's nothing between us now. Does it bother you that Lance is white? It's got to be some other explanation on why you're flipping out every time you see me with another guy."

"For one, I care about you."

"Yeah, right."

"No, I do, and I mean, guys talk. You gon' be going up to school here in a minute—you want everybody to be saying you a ho—"

She took her hand and slapped me across my face. Why couldn't I find the words to tell her how I felt? Why didn't I even know how I felt? Why was this so confusing? She meant something to me. How come it couldn't come across the right way?

"I hate that you're sticking your nose in between all of my happiness. I'm coming to school here, Perry, but I'm not coming for you to mandate my every move. It's like you don't want me, but you don't want anyone else to have me."

All I could see was her lips moving as if they were inviting me to come and kiss them or something. So I took my head, pressed both my hands on her cheeks, pulled her head toward mine, and let her know who she wanted to be with. I had no intentions other than that kiss, but I knew I wanted it to last and last in both her mind and mine. If I couldn't verbally express how I felt, certainly I could show her, and at that moment I was feeling her with my spirit, because I was speaking in tongues.

"Perry, I got to go," Savoy said as she ended our wonderful moment together, but before I could do anything, she grabbed her purse, headed out of my bedroom, out the front door, and left me there alone. I sank to my bed. It was ten thirty and I had wondered what I had done. If Savoy had feelings for Lance, I certainly confused her. Just when I thought the day couldn't get any worse, my cell phone rang. With dread, I picked up the phone. It was too late to talk to anybody, and when I realized it was my folks' number, inwardly I was agitated. Should I answer the phone, or should I not get it? They probably just called to check on me, to make sure I still wasn't out partying. Before I was about to let the answering machine get it, I decided to answer. "Hello?" I tried not to sound too excited or to sound like I was in trouble, but I tried not to sound too sleepy either, because they knew I wouldn't be asleep at ten something.

Frantically my mother said, "Okay, Perry, I need you to listen to me."

"Mom, what's wrong? Damarius is out of jail and everything, right?"

"Honey, you saw that TV chase?" she said.

"Yeah, he's okay right?"

"I don't know, baby, but that's not what I'm talking about."

When she took a deep breath, I did as well. What in the world was she about to tell me? Was everything okay? Instead of sending myself into a frenzy, I just prayed to the Lord, "Please just let me be able to handle whatever she throws at me."

"What is it, Mom?"

"It's your dad, son."

"What's wrong with him? What, what's going on with him?"

"He came home at around six o'clock and basically said that the dealership was closing."

"What?" I said, completely shocked.

"Son, I don't know everything that's going on but it looks pretty bad. He's getting a lot of pressure from Corporate and he was very, very upset."

"So, where is he now? Put him on the phone. I want to talk to him."

"That's just it, he said he was out of here and went to talk to his mom. He said he's letting down his father's legacy and that he needed to talk to her."

"He's up here?" I said, knowing that Conyers was considered the greater Atlanta area.

"I don't know. I know how to get in touch with her but her phone just kept ringing busy, and I'm worried. It's almost eleven o'clock and I haven't heard from your father and he's not even picking up his phone. It's just not like him, Perry. I don't know . . ."

"Mom, calm down. I'll go check on him. You don't need to be stressed out."

"I know if he goes up there and has a meeting with those people, everything's going to be okay, but he won't listen to me, he just won't listen to me. He just hightailed it out of here."

"Ma, I'm a go over to Grandma's and check on everything."

"Sweetie, it's late. I don't even want you ripping and running the streets yourself."

"Mom, you called me. I'm on this side of town. It's better for me to go check it out than for you to be worried up there in Augusta."

"Well, keep your cell phone on, sweetie. I need to know you're okay, too."

"Yes, ma'am. I'll touch base with you once I find out something; I'm sure Dad's fine."

"Oh, Perry!"

When I hung up the phone, I grabbed my keys. Deuce was walking in the door.

"Man, what's up, you got to let Lance go. Y'all got to put this rift aside."

"Look seriously, this has nothing to do with Lance, I'll be back in a little while. I got to go check on my grandma."

"You're grandma lives around here?"

"Not too far from here. She's up the road, over in your neck of the woods, up in Conyers."

"You want me to roll with you, since it's late?"

"Nah, I've been going there for years. I head up 20 and get off the exit; she's not too far off of that. I appreciate your concern, my man."

"Alright, man, keep your cell phone on and I'll keep base with you; holla at me if you need something."

"Will do."

I couldn't believe my mom had come to me with one of her problems. I so badly wanted to be the hero and save things for her, but my father losing his dealership, dang, that hurt me to the core. First of all, I had to find him, and when I did, I needed to let him know the pain he deserved to rightly feel would go away, but I wasn't even sure if I believed that, so how in the heck could I convince my father of it?

When I got in my car, I dialed my grandmother. Like my mom said, it just rang busy. That was not a settling sign. Headed 20 East, the highways were isolated. It was like more of the traffic was going toward Atlanta and I was on the interstate by myself, which was fine with me except it gave me a reason to go a little faster. Thankfully I spotted a cop and slowed things down. The last thing I needed to do was join Damarius behind bars. It's not like my dad didn't already have enough on his plate to worry about. When I got to Conyers, though, a light was on at my grandmother's place; I knocked on the door pretty forcefully and she said, "I'm coming, I'm coming! Junior baby, is that you?"

"Yes, ma'am, I'm looking for my dad. Mom said he came down here."

"Yeah, he was down here not too long ago all upset. Said he let me down and needed to go talk to his father."

"Grandma, how is he supposed to do that?"

"I don't know, baby, before I could talk any sense into him, he was gone. I figured he went over to the cemetery or something. I've been praying for him, but every time your dad would get all hot under the collar, I'd give him a little space and he'd calm his little self down on back to the house. So I figured that's what he's going to do, gon' out there talk to his dad and then come on back so I could feed him some chitlins and collard greens."

"Grandma, how do I get to the cemetery from here? Do they have lights out there?"

She gave me directions and told me I'd be okay. She confirmed all the dead people would leave me alone, but there was something a little eerie about heading to a cemetery at eleven o'clock at night, but I had to go. I had to see if my dad was there, and sure enough, when I went up the road, I saw his demo car. There weren't any lights out there, but his car lights were on. I could see his body leaning over his father's headstone. I wasn't trying to startle him, but the noise of my car never moved him to see what was coming. That in itself bothered me. My father was always very astute at his surroundings. When I called his name and took the flashlight I kept in my glove department, which my mom always made me carry, I could see his face was filled with tears.

"Son, I done messed up trying to be a hero; trying to help others I messed up my family, all that my dad built. I've let him down."

My dad grabbed a hold of his father's headstone. I had never seen him weeping in my life. Even the day we put his father in the ground my dad held strong, and now it was as if he was letting go of the pent-up sadness he never released back then.

"My dad just cared about his family, Perry. That's all he cared about. He left me over the estate and the dealership because he knew I knew how to preserve that and I let my pride get in the way. I tried to take on a conglomerate, a company who don't care nothing about us black folks. I wanted them to walk when they were happy to crawl. Why couldn't that be enough? Why'd I have to risk everything and now lose everything? Dad, I'm *soo* sorry."

My father never said he wanted to join his dad at the moment, but I could tell a part of him had given up, not because he was showing emotion, but because the hope in his heart had gone out like the flame of life from every other person other than him and me surrounding us. But he wasn't dead. He could live to change things. Somehow, some way, I had to give him back his hope. The only way I knew how to do that was to ask God to help me pour faith into my father. While he wept and cried some more, I turned around and looked up at the black sky and said silently, "Lord, you got to help me help my dad." Then it dawned on me; I remembered my grandfather's favorite hymn, "Pass Me Not, O Gentle Savior," and I just start saying, "Pass me not, hear my humble cry; while on others thou art calling, do not pass me by," and I said it a little louder the next time and then a little louder, and before I knew it, the man who was hugging the tombstone was now hugging me.

So I said to him, "God has not forgotten you. Circumstances might not look good right now, Dad, but you got to trust that God can make it better."

"I don't know, son, I don't think he can make me better. I messed up, my dad said not to be too prideful, and I was. I just can't do this anymore. I just can't."

I almost lost it when my father revealed the shiny silver gun in his hand. He pushed me back. I started shaking. I bit my lip and said, "Lord, you got to help me now, my dad's losing it, he can't kill himself. Help him see he has self-worth, he needs to be restored with what matters."

~ 10 ~

Glorifying God Always

"Dad, what are you doing?" I said as I saw the steel gun in my dad's hand. I took a step toward him. "Please, Dad, give me the gun, please."

"Son, you need to back up. Back up."

I had been so used to obeying him all my life, he knew what was good for me all my life, but now I couldn't honor his wishes. We were in reverse roles—he had to listen to me. I couldn't talk like a scared child. I had to dry my tears. I had to let him understand that I was right. Feeling worse than if I had a real ulcer, I brushed off all my insecurities, knowing that the Lord was with me, and though this was uncomfortable, I'd get through it victoriously.

"Alright, Dad, I know that you feel like maybe you have made a wrong decision, but the only perfect man that walked this earth was Jesus Christ. We all fall short; Granddad put you in charge for a reason."

"If he could see me now, he'd be *soo* ashamed. I just need to end this."

"No, Dad. No! He'd want you to learn from this and rise up better from it."

"You weren't supposed to find me here, Perry. I need you

to go on away, son. Just pretend like you never saw me, okay?"

"Dad, you know I can't do that. Mom needs you, Payton needs you."

"They'll be alright."

"Dad, look at me." I took a couple steps toward him and I placed my hand on his shoulders. "I need you."

"You weren't supposed to see me broken like this. What have I done now?"

"Dad, you're living your life. You're going through something that hurts. Why can't you be human? Why does every black man have to be so strong that his family can't see him suffer? Then in the end we have to pick up the pieces when we could have helped you fix things along the way?"

"I don't know. It's just how it's always been."

"But for our family, it can't be like that any longer."

When he wasn't looking, I knocked the gun out of his hand.

"Perry, what . . . wh . . . what are you doing? I . . . I . . ."

"Dad, let it go."

"I got to find it. Where is it . . . where?"

The gun was behind his dad's tombstone, but I couldn't let him know that. If he couldn't find out where it was, then I was successful. He had to hear me out on this.

"Dad, I've admired you all my life and I admire you right now."

"You admire me, son. I'm all broken."

"You're broken because you had a heart that cared about other people. So what if things got a little steamy and they're turning the heat up on you now. It's like you tell me in a football situation, just look at this like you're down by a couple of points, but there's still some time on the clock."

"I don't want to quit, son."

"You can't quit, Dad."

He fell into my arms and we dropped to the ground. It was actually symbolic because we were on top of his father's grave, three generations immersed in the dirt, but just like the soil, it was planting time. Okay, my dad would have to start over with some things. I didn't have all the answers but I knew we could figure it out together.

"I'm sorry, son."

"Dad, you owe me no apologies."

"Thank you for being here."

"I love you, Dad. I'll never forget that you didn't give up on life. Thank you, it'd be hard for us to make it without you."

He squeezed me tighter. I just prayed, "Lord, I thank you for my dad, thank you for his dad's life, and I know life gets crazy and we can't control everything that happens but we can bring it to you and we know that you can fix things. Thank you for leading me here tonight, for allowing me and my dad to bond. His life is so important to me and I'm glad he knows that I love him and you love him. The plan you have for his life isn't done yet."

"God," my father stepped in, "thank you for my son. I've been so worried for him to find you, it looks like he is a little closer to you than I am these days and that's a good thing. Tonight it's shown me what's important and that's trusting you with the tough stuff. Take my life, Lord, take the mess that I have made of it and help me fix it and get this boy on back to college. Stay with him Lord, I love you. I love him, I love my dad. In Jesus' name we pray, Amen.

"I miss my dad, son," my father said to me as we walked away from the grave site.

"He thought you were a great son, Dad. I know he's looking down on you proud from Heaven."

"Well, if anything, he's looking down proud of you. Just like I'm proud of you right now. You really came through for me tonight. The gun, where's the gun?"

"Dad, don't worry about that. I got it."

"Son, you don't need to be walking around with no gun. It's registered to me and everything."

"I got it, Dad. You know I'm not giving it back to you."

"That's fair."

When I got in my car, I just thanked God. The night could have gone so much worse, but the Lord gave us favor. I knew my mom was worried so I called her.

Her voice was anything but calm. "Please tell me you called him, Perry, son, talk to me. Did you find your dad?"

"Yes, ma'am. He's okay, Mom. You do not need to worry."

"So, he wasn't upset, he's good? Well, where'd you find him?"

"Mom, I don't want you worrying about any of that, he's good."

Some kind of bond between my father and I had happened that night. There was no way I'd ever tell anyone what I had witnessed. The father-son loyalty had kicked in like a mug. My dad had let me into his world and allowed me to help him. I would never reveal the outcome of tonight's events.

When we got to his mom's house, she started asking questions as well. I was able to let my father know with eye contact that I had his back, but Grandma wasn't stupid. She knew her son was at his wit's end. She stepped into the kitchen after giving us some chitlins and hot sauce and said, "Son, I just want to tell you, your dad wasn't always that perfect. Before he got the corporate dealership, he had a little ol' used car lot. Money started coming in so fast he was spending it before he was paying his bills. We lost everything. I had four small children to take care of. I couldn't go get no job, but he got a banker to get him another loan, and once he got another chance, he made sure he never let us down again. And son, sometimes you have to lose everything to gain true wealth and the way you two chummed your way in here seems like whatever you two went through tonight might have been worth it.

She left out and gave us some time alone. My dad reached out for my hand and said, "These chitlins are good. Momma don't like fixing them. They stink and they messy."

"They are tasty, Dad." We exchanged small talk.

"Listen, son, I just wanted to let you know that, umm, Mom was right. I went through a lot tonight and my boy helped me through it. I don't know or claim to understand all of God's methods, but I'm certainly thankful that he brought me to my knees so you could help me stand. I love you."

"I love you, too, Dad."

He didn't know how he was going to rebuild his empire, but in the midst of being on the bottom, he was grateful. I loved seeing that lesson. I knew I needed to rebuild it on myself one day.

"Thank you, God," I thought as I woke up the next morning realizing that I still had a father. I so wanted the events of the previous night to be a dream, but it wasn't. However, it didn't matter—the outcome was a jubilant one. And that's all that really mattered. My Heavenly Father gave my worldly father a new outlook on life, and I quickly grabbed the phone and called my dad to make sure he was still upbeat.

"Son, you don't have to touch base with me every day," he said.

"I know, Dad, I . . . I just wanted to hear your voice this morning."

"You need to make sure you take care of that gun."

"Yes, sir, I got it."

"I'm thinking clearly again and the last thing I want to do is put steel in your hands."

"Dad, you don't need to worry about me, and like you're telling me, I don't need to worry about you."

"But it's to know that we still care about each other, right?"

"Yes, sir, that's a good thing."

"Y'all got practice today?"

"Yes. Yeah, it's media day. Freshman got to talk to the press and stuff."

"Oh, you'll do great. I'll look for a spot with you on there."

"Son, thank you!" I heard my mom scream from the back.

I was the last one out of the apartment. Deuce, Collin, and Lance had dipped out. I must admit though the peace and quiet was heavenly, when we had to meet with the marketing director, and I would have liked to be back in bed. And the way Lance partied, I was surprised to see him up this morning, although he was getting his groove on. It was amazing how he was able to take care of business. Of course, I'd never tell him that. I wasn't sure if we'd ever click. As I walked toward the athletic building, I just spent more time with God. I'd been through so much I was only hoping the drama was over—girl drama, racial issues, burying a friend, physical frailties. Just having to go through all of that, a normal person probably would have been insane. However, place any normal person with God and what would seem like crazy, He would make normal. I could only look up at the beautiful blue sky and say, "Thank you, Lord, for loving me enough to be here in the midst of the craziness. I know I got a lot of haters, but I don't care because, Lord, you make my skin thick. However, Lord, I do want to bond with my teammates without compromising who I am. Show me a way to make that happen."

"Perry, there you are," Anne Jamison, the marketing director, came up to me and said. "All the press wants to talk to you. They've already asked the other players all they wanted to know and I have stalled them as long as I can. You ready to talk?"

I just shrugged my shoulder like "Yeah, I guess."

Tech's hive had everything—tons of computers for the players to play on, three big-screen TVs, some couches to lounge on, and an area where media could ask us questions behind a podium.

Mrs. Jamison pushed me behind the mike, and before I knew it, tons of questions were being hurled at me from reporters, both local and national, from television and radio. She came up behind me and said, "You just point to one of them and then answer the question without everybody asking at the same time."

I pointed to a guy with an ESPN hat on.

"Thanks, Perry," he said. "I'm Macon Fraizer from ESPN. How does it feel to finally be in college? Tech has a great recruiting class, but it's far superior with you here. Your teammates treating you well?"

Now what kind of question was that? Before I could answer, I looked past the crowd and saw my class of freshmen standing off to the side staring at me. I wasn't going to lie but I wasn't going to let on that we had problems.

So I tried to give a politically correct answer and said, "It's great for all of us to be here and get a chance to gel. As you mentioned, Macon, we've got talent overflowing with this Tech freshman class and I'm just happy to be a part of it."

I pointed to another reporter and he asked another controversial question. "Saxon Lee is another great receiver but clearly his skills and athletic abilities don't compare to yours even, though we talked to him and he thinks that he is the best." Reporters chuckled. "Coaches said probably only one of you will start, and we know who it is. How is it going between the two of you off the field?"

"Umm, actually we haven't even thought about it. We're both competitive, though if you ask Saxon, he'll say he's going to play, and if you ask me, I'll say I'm going to play. So maybe it's upperclassmen you have to talk to? Coach might change his mind and have two freshmen on the field come fall."

"What makes you such a special athlete, Perry?" a female reporter asked me.

"Well, I appreciate the compliment, ma'am, but I just consider myself a football player. I get out there and I work hard and people talk about the reach in my stride. I guess you got to thank the Lord for giving me big hands and big feet and my parents, too." More laughs.

When I was done answering about twenty more questions, they still had more to throw at me. Mrs. Jamison came in and said, "That'll be all, guys. Perry has to head to workouts now."

"You did very well," she said to me as we walked past the guys. I thought I was getting ready to practice like Mrs. Jamison had told the reporters, but she said loudly, "You need to come with me. ESPN actually wants to do a TV interview and *Sports Illustrated* wants to talk to you now."

"He just thinks he's something," I heard one of the defensive guys I didn't know say.

I walked behind Mrs. Jamison, my head down a little low. I didn't want people to think I ever asked for the media to play me up. I mean, I was used to it from high school but it was like insane this day.

"You're the biggest recruit we've had come here in years. It might get a little crazy when it comes to the media, but you know the rule—only talk to the press through the stuff I set up, okay?"

"Yeah, I got it, but you don't have to set up so much for me. I mean, there are tons of other freshmen; let someone else have a chance. I tried to beef up all of the players."

"Just so you know, I'm not playing favorites but again your skills, your stats, the hype about you, of course, everyone wants to talk to you, and until that changes on the field, which of course is not what we want, we want you to get out there and perform. You might as well get used to it. You speak eloquently. You don't have to worry about embarrassing yourself or anything."

"No, no, that's not a problem with me."

"So your teammates are getting to you, huh?"

"I'm just not used to people craving for attention."

"Well, I heard you mention the Lord in one of your questions. You got him to thank."

Later on that day when all the interviews were over, I joined the rest of my class in the athletic cafeteria. It was like a scene out of a prison movie, of something where a new inmate came and no one wanted him to join them at their table. I got all kinds of crazy looks. But Deuce had my back and motioned for me to come over and sit with him.

"What's up, guy?" I said as we slapped hands.

"You had a busy day, boy. I'm a have to get me some of them interviews to get out of workouts."

"Trust me, boy, I would have rather been running fa'sho then running my mouth, you know?"

"I hear you."

"So, all your teammates been talking about me, huh?" I said, trying to get a feel for what I was really dealing with.

This was new for me. Even though I was great in high school, my team was always supportive. I mean, there was one jerk here or there, but they were the minority and no one ever let my status make them feel inferior. But here it seemed that they were out for my blood.

"Man, you got to learn how to shrug off the negative folks."

"How in the heck am I supposed to do that?"

"Every door that's open to you is one that the Lord opened. If He wants to shut it down, then He will. Don't apologize for the blessings that God gives. You just got to graciously take 'em. Keep doing your thang. He'll work out everyone else's response. Eat up, we got two days."

"Thanks, guy."

It did feel good to have a real friend. Deuce was right—I needed to be grateful.

When we were out on the field for the second workout, the press and media had not gone. This time it wasn't me they were in awe of. Deuce was throwing down on his routes. He was not only zipping and zapping through the drills but he was also catching out of the backfield step by step with me and he wasn't even a receiver. A couple of times Lance threw it up high and he went into the air and caught it. Lance threw it low and Deuce caught it and let his body hit the ground, but not the pigskin. Saxon did everything he could to try and get the attention of the media, but when they were looking, he dropped his passes. Like Deuce said, I didn't have to wish anything bad on anybody. The Lord would humble us all. When practice was over, Anne led Deuce over to the media.

"I guess you're not the man anymore," Saxon said behind my ear.

Why would he think I cared that Deuce was getting high-lighted? He showed out in practice and ran circles around the rest of us. He was my boy. I wanted him to get recognized. I just wasn't expecting one reporter to say, "Shucks, maybe we overestimated our interview with Perry Skky Jr. this morning. Maybe he's not the one to be looking out for. Maybe Deuce, it's you. Any comments?"

"Perry is a competitor. He makes us all compete at our best. I think you need to be looking out for the Yellow Jackets. We plan to make a big presence in the ACC this year."

I liked Deuce. I couldn't be upset that the press was trying to play the two of us against each other. We had a neat friendship going and I knew neither he nor I would do anything to ruin it. Watching Deuce give his interview, I had to admit to myself that I felt a little weird. Never had any player gotten attention over me, and although it was well deserved, I needed to figure out how I felt about that. All of a sudden Saxon came up to me and said, "Oh, so it doesn't feel good, huh, seeing somebody else get the press's attention?"

"What are you talking about, man? I'm fine with it. You're tripping."

"Naw, bruh, I can see that look in your eye."

"What look?" I said to him.

"The look of fear, of disdain, of he's about to take my position of power and influence away from me. I know that look. You've been the man for so long you don't even know the feeling to be intimidated by another player."

I didn't know what look Saxon was talking about that I possessed, but I knew that I had no room for envy in my heart; Deuce was one of the finest running backs I had ever come across. He credited his talent to natural ability that God gave him that he had worked hard to refine. How could I be upset about that? Not wanting to show the wrong emotions or say the wrong thing, I stayed to myself pretty much most of the evening.

The next day at practice I was in full stride ready to stay in my own lane and do my own thing, not be focused on how good or bad someone else was coming along. But the harder I saw Deuce working at drills, the more I wanted to push through my own pain and show up just as much. We were going toe for toe there for a moment, and then when I planted my left foot down too hard on a catch, I fell to the ground in pain. My shin that was busted in the attack on the beach wasn't healed enough to take all the full-blown press I was applying to it and it gave. Trainers rushed out on the field toward me. I wanted media attention and I was getting it all right. Tons of cameras were flashing at my downfall. Deuce even came over to help me up and I didn't feel as if I deserved his genuine concern.

"Get back out there and practice, man. Don't worry about me," I said as I got carted off the field.

The trainer came out to me and told me it looked like I'd be out for two weeks, and I was so bummed out about that because we'd be heading into training camp and all of the veterans would be coming back. Last thing I wanted to be doing was sitting on the sideline when the team was in full court workouts. Everybody had come in, gotten dressed, and gone upstairs to get something to eat, but no one had come to see about me. The trainer just wanted me to relax for a minute as they monitored to make sure my leg wasn't worse than they thought. I didn't want visitors, but somebody checking in on me would've been okay. Just when I had given up hope, Deuce knocked on the trainer's door.

"Hey, man, you got a sec?"

"Yeah, man, come on in. They just got me relaxing, icing my knee and stuff."

"I just wanted to talk to you, make sure you're all right."

"You ain't have to do that. I know you hungry."

"You need me to bring you something to eat?"

"Naw, they're taking care of it. They're bringing me a tray down. They don't want me to move for a minute. I just can't believe I hurt my knee again."

"Yeah, you were really giving it a lot like you were trying to keep up with me or something. What's up with that, Perry?"

"I don't know, Deuce. I don't want to lie to you and say I'm not a little intimidated, but you've been making me work extra hard. I've been asking myself the same question. 'Why was I pushing myself more than I needed to?' Saxon called me out yesterday and said I had a little bit of the green eye, said I had monster syndrome when you were being attacked by those reporters."

"There's no truth to that, right? You know you still the man? I told everybody so."

"Yeah, I heard what you said, but they still were interested in talking to you. I mean rightly, so you showed your butt out there, man."

"So, what are you not saying?"

"I don't know, this whole thing is kind of new for me. Seeing that I was always man on the team, it seems that I may be sharing that role. Honestly I'd like nothing better than to share it with someone down like you. Maybe I'm afraid to admit to myself that I'm really not capable of being somebody's friend. 'Cause if I was truly your buddy, I wouldn't be sweating you getting some spotlight, you know?"

"Man, you're human. You know I've been going full speed like that because I've been trying to keep wit' you. You bring out the best in me and what's wrong with me pulling out the best in you?"

"Everything when I'm not ready to do it."

"Well, that's true."

We laughed.

"So you think that's healthy, me feeling a little intimidated?"

"Healthy, I'm not no psychologist, Perry, but I mean, I think it's normal. Teammates should bounce off energy from one another and maybe you having to sit down for a second is allowing you to see that this is going to be a team effort. I gotta run like heck and you got to catch some passes out yo' behind for us to show off, ya' know? We gon' do this thing up for Tech this year."

"Whether it's me showing out or you showing out, I think we'll both get ours in the end. God's gon' take care of it. So even in my injury I need to be thankful."

"Yeah, sometimes He pulls us down to pull us back up and I don't know if I would have been able to tell you I'm motivated by you 'til I saw that I was doing the same thing to you. Got you all messed up. I feel bad about that."

"I'm just learning in everything, though, to be up front and honest. That's the only way I think that God can use me and mold me and make me better."

"Thanks, man. This is new for me, too, but you're making sense in everything. We need to be glorying God always."

~ 11 ~
Being a Gentleman

I had only known two people in the last year to pass on: my dear grandfather and my high school friend. Ironically, though, it would be only a week apart before I found myself in another cemetery visiting another grave. Although Ciara wasn't gone for a complete year, Damarius was out of jail and called and asked if I'd come down and join the crew to put flowers on her grave. It was her birthday. Since it was the weekend and coaches wanted me to take it easy on my leg, getting away from all the Georgia Tech action for a weekend didn't sound so bad. But also seeing my dad in full swing again was something I was looking forward to so I hopped in the car and headed east to Augusta. Cole and I had talked and said this would not be a somber occasion, but since I came off the interstate right to the cemetery and met the crew, I walked upon all kinds of somber faces. Cole was holding Brianna's hand. Damarius was kneeling down with water coming from his eyes, and then I saw Tori. She and I had had so much history it broke my heart to see her sad about her friend. I knew we all believed she was in a much better place than we were—I mean she was with God—but still even months later it still affected each of us in our own small ways.

"Hey, guys," I said as I walked up on them. Damarius got

up and came over and hugged me. There was no way I could minimize his anguish and all that he was feeling. But I was happy to know that I put smiles on all four of their faces.

"Ciara wouldn't want us to be sad, y'all," I said sensitively as I tried to respect everyone's feelings, placing my bouquet on her grave.

"Naw, I mean, you're right. She would want us to look out for each other and keep doing the right thing, and I guess that's why I am so emotional right now. She'd kick my butt if she knew I was in jail messing with Jayboe."

"Oh, so what, it taught you something?" I said in a shocked tone. I definitely didn't want to start a rift with Damarius but his acts had been so juvenile hanging with a drug dealer when he knew he was about to rob a convenience store. What was he thinking? I guess that was the point—he didn't care about wrecking his life, but now at the foot of Ciara's grave, he wanted more for himself.

"I'm a get it together, Perry, I am. I think I will pass the graduation test, I really, really been studying hard. Jail ain't no joke and I don't want to live my life like that."

"So what about the charges?" I asked, caring about my friend.

"There was a videotape. Can you believe it?" Cole said as he came from behind and hugged Damarius around the neck. "The boy is cleared. They saw the whole thing. He wasn't even involved."

"But I got to testify against Jayboe."

"You gon' do that?" I said, knowing the risk.

"Ciara's life is gone; if he takes me out, I'll be better with her anyway. But if I don't stand up like a man, what will my life stand for?"

We slapped hands and gave a nice hug to each other. I was so proud of Damarius. I only hoped he would continue sticking to the right plan to keep himself on track.

"Hey, Perry!" Tori said, looking real cute.

"Hey, lady, good to see you," I said, remembering times when she didn't keep herself up as much as she used to.

Brianna stood by her girl and said, "Y'all we need to pray and then go get something to eat. Damarius you can ride with us, and Tori, you can ride with Perry. We'll follow each other to Hal's barbeque. Cool? Ciara would love us to chow down some chicole."

"Yeah, everybody always did love my grandma's drink."

It was cool that her friend was pushing the two of us together. I hadn't seen Tori in a while, so after we paid our last respects to Ciara, we ended our time with her singing "Happy Birthday" off-key. We all laughed and got into the two different cars. Instinctively I went to open up the door.

"You didn't have to do that."

"Oh, I don't mind being a gentleman. It's good to see you looking good," I said.

"I could also ride with them. You know, Brianna is still trying to play the matchmaking game with me and you."

"I told you I'd always care about you, girl. Anyways we can chat. It's good to see you, girl." I didn't want any awkward moments between us so I just jumped into the conversation and asked how she'd been and she went on to tell me about her cheerleading drama, her new job at the mall, and how she and Brianna were closer now after Ciara's passing. I wanted to ask her about guys, not that I felt like a big brother or anything, and I certainly wasn't jealous like with Savoy, but I didn't know how to talk about the subject so I said nothing. Then things did get awkward, and then things got really awkward when she said, "You know I still care about you, right?"

"Honestly, I hoped you'd be over me," I told her.

"You'll always be the man in my book, Perry."

"Well, now I'm up in college and a whole bunch of people that got it going on. For real I'm not the big hero."

"But you're kind and gentle and care about others. You care about me. I mean, you were my first. How am I ever going to put that aside? Though I don't want to make you feel uncomfortable, I'm not trying to start anything up again, I mean, I know you're a big college boy and all I just . . . I don't know. I wanted to tell you that I pray for you all the time now."

"Tori, that means a lot." I stroked her hand, hoping that she wouldn't take my gesture the wrong way, but I didn't know how to respond other than to be me. She knew there was no future for us. She was right—I was in a whole other world—heck, she still lived at her parents' house. I had my own place. Though we were only a year apart, it seemed like we were in two different worlds. She was still a baby, her parents' baby, and I was a grown man saving my dad. Images of her wanting to give up on her life would forever haunt me. I guess I had fallen for Tori because she was so strong, and when I had found her so weak that she wanted to break, I just couldn't see my way to putting the pieces of our relationship back together ever.

"How will I ever get over you? It's so clear that you had moved on from being into me," she admitted as she looked out the passenger side window.

I huffed, not wanting to disregard her feelings. I wasn't an overly sensitive schmuck, but I wasn't a jerk either. I wasn't flattered that she couldn't stop thinking about me, but I wasn't unmoved by it either.

"You know, I hurt my leg again," I said, changing the subject.

"You hurt your leg again? Are you going to be okay? Are you going to be able to play this season?"

"I don't know. Honestly I hope so. It's weird having it so tender and reinjuring it by some circumstance or I'm putting too much pressure on it before it's ready, reinjuring it that way. I guess I understand when you say things don't go your way, working out the way you want, but I'm just trying to learn how to take this day by day. Maybe you should do the same thing too. I pray to God to show me how to take care of my physical ailments and maybe you should ask Him to heal your heart."

"I appreciate that," she said, looking over at me. "You're so cool, you could be such a joke and take advantage of all that I was saying, but you won't and maybe that's why you're so hard to get over."

"Yeah, but you deserve someone that cares about you as much as you care about them."

"Are you and that Savoy girl working out?"

"Honestly, Tori, I don't know what is going on with that."

"She'll be a fool not to pay you any attention."

"She ain't thinking about me and that's cool. If it's for us, it'll be in the cards. I guess what I'm trying say is God's got a plan for us and some guy, the right guy, is going to come along and make your heart feel better than I ever could. Right now it's not that time. You just talked about cheerleading and you and Brianna hanging out and you're a senior. Trust me when I say, 'Your time is going to fly by.' Enjoy it. Be smart. Do your thing, and if you need me, I'm here for you. You know that."

"You know you're killing me, you're such a great guy."

"And you're a great girl. Friends?"

"Friends."

Then we parked at Hal's Barbeque, leaving all the worries, the cares, the woes, the stresses, the strains, and the negative thoughts behind us.

Sunday after church I was happy to head back to school. Being at home didn't prove challenging. In fact, it was quite refreshing to get my father smiling all over the place. He had

big changes ahead with him selling the dealership and looking at other ways to make ends meet, and his joy was restored. My mom was in her element, too, cooking up a big
spread like it was Thanksgiving for her two favorite men.
They were even going at each other as if they were on a honey-
moon or something. Yep, heading back to my new home was
refreshing.

One of my favorite pastimes besides watching films, working out, or playing football was going to the movies all alone.
My favorite genres were comedy and action. So instead of
going directly to the apartment and spending the rest of the
day with knuckleheads, I decided to take in a flick. Atlantic
Station, a new Arizona-type outdoor shopping complex, was
right near Tech. As I stood in line to purchase a ticket for the
karate action film, I thought I heard somebody calling my
name. It was a female voice I wasn't familiar with.

"Perry, is that you, Perry?" When I turned around, it was a
blonde that seemed familiar but something about her seemed
eerie, too.

"Do I know you?" I said in a cautious tone.

"I'm Anna Pond."

I still didn't know who she was talking about.

"From the summer in Hilton Head. You saved me."

Then I could have had a V8 hit me upside the head or
something. How could I forget that face? It was dark, she had
a bloody face and all, but yeah, it was Anna Pond, the white
chick from the beach.

"You do remember me, right?" she asked.

"Yeah, I do remember. How you doing?" I said, not wanting to be rude as I moved from the ticket line to head inside.
She looked behind me and in front of me. I didn't know if I
had something on my clothes or something.

"What, what's going on?" I asked.

"No, it just seems that you're by yourself. I don't want to be presumptuous. Were you about to go to a movie?"

"Yeah, I'm just relaxing." I looked behind her and saw three other girls with sorority letters across their shirts.

"Clearly you're not alone?"

"Well, I'm with my girls but I can go tell them to see something else. Maybe see what you're going to see if you want some company."

"Oh naw, you don't have to do that." Trying not to get myself into anything crazy.

"For everything you've done for me this summer, the least I could do is buy you some popcorn and a Snickers bar. I mean football players do eat junk food, right?"

With her friends looking on, I didn't want to embarrass her and tell her that I wasn't up for any kind of date, but before I could get that out, even in a quiet way, she said, "Look, it's no big thing. We're not considering this a date or anything. We're going to catch a movie together. It's no use to go by yourself if I'm here. I didn't even want to see what they were seeing. Some romantic comedy—what's the fun in that?"

"Yeah, alright, cool."

She asked me to wait right there for her to exchange her ticket and talk to her girls. They smiled at me and gave me the thumbs-up and stuff. I don't know what she told them, but I clearly needed to make her understand for real this was strictly platonic. While I waited my cell phone rang.

"Hey, Mom."

"I'm just checking to make sure you got back to Atlanta all right."

"Yeah, I'm straight."

"But you're not at your place. I just called there. Your roommates said they hadn't seen you."

"Awh, I'm checking out a movie."

"I'm back," Anna said loudly.

"Who's back? You out with some little girl? Some fast girl. See, I told your daddy we didn't need to rush you out of here."

"I'm not being any faster than you and Daddy were, Momma."

"Yeah right, son, me and your father are married, okay? Do we need to get in the car and come to Atlanta to get you straight? You know those little girls are just happy they landed themselves a football player they think going somewhere. They don't even see color, they see green, and you don't have a dime to your name. Be careful, boy, you hear me?"

"Yes ma'am, we're just going to a movie."

"Alright, well, we'll touch base with you later on tonight." I hung up the phone.

"Was that your mom?"

"Yeah, and why were you talking all loud? That could have been—"

"What, a girlfriend?" she teased.

"Just be cool when you see me on the phone like that, dang. I wouldn't mess you up."

"We're just friends. How could you mess me up. Any girl could understand that, right?" she teased as I followed her into the theater.

I had to admit for a guy who wasn't into white girls, Anna Pond cleaned up nicely. Her beautiful blond hair and pearly whites and fine tanned skin would make any man breathing excited.

"I knew you were going to Tech," I said to her as we sat in the theater before the previews played. "But you're here sort of early."

"Yeah, I'm here for sorority rush. After everything that happened last month, my parents thought it best that I go ahead and get out of Bluffton."

"So you seem to be coping well. Did they catch the guy?" I didn't want to bring up any bad memories, but I went through a lot because of the dude that raped her. Knowing that he got what was coming to him was something I needed to hear.

"They caught him. He confessed to taking things too far and they gave him community service and a couple of days in juve."

"That's good."

"I still can't believe you didn't press charges against the guys who hurt you."

"You know nobody even knows about that whole incident, so—"

"Oh, no, no. I not going to bring it up to anybody or nothing. I'm just excited I ran into you. Sometimes when I think about that night, you're the only bright spot out of it all."

Ironically, nothing about that night was bright for me although Anna did speak up when it finally counted. We were at the same school and had been brought together by fate. I tried not being so tense. When the movie was over, her friends were nowhere around. She called their numbers but nobody answered.

"They must be still in their movie. Umm, I'm sort of hungry. Can I get you something to eat?" she asked.

"Naw, I'm straight. I'm a get back to my dorm."

"Awh, Perry, you got to eat something."

"Naw, seriously. My mom made a big spread before I left home."

"You said you lived in Augusta. That was a couple hours' ride. We just sat in a two-hour movie, and you ate—what?— four hours ago? Come on, you got to be hungry. Or what about dessert? There's the ice cream shop over there."

I couldn't believe I let this chick talk me into "hanging." She wasn't a dumb ditzy blonde or anything but she wasn't my type. Though my uncle Percy was married to a white lady, I'd always seen my mom and my sister and my grandma as beautiful Nubian queens. Maybe my time at Tech would change that. But the only thing a blonde could do was point me to the chocolate. A few people looked at us as we sat in the ice cream parlor. I don't know if it was me being paranoid or if what I was thinking they were thinking was true.

"You uncomfortable around me?" Anna asked.

"That was a joke, uncomfortable?" I said. "No."

"Well, why do you seem so tense? Can I be honest with you, Perry?"

"Sure."

"Ever since that crazy night on the beach, I have been seeing your picture everywhere, and I've never been attracted to a black man before but it's something about you that's uniquely special. And running into you like this today, getting a chance to connect with you before all the girls come back to school. I don't know, maybe we can give this friendship thing a chance."

"Being friends is cool. I'm not really looking for anything more. I don't want you to feel like you owe me something from this summer. I was in the right place and God put me in the right place to help you."

"Well, don't say no on us before we even get a chance."

"Well, I don't want to mislead you."

"I respect you for that," she said. Thankfully her girlfriends showed up. I made small pleasantries with them and made a quick exit.

"Hey, Skky," Saxon said as he knocked on our door the next day. "Look, since you don't have to work out and some of us do—my sister is coming up here to run the track and bringing some of my stuff. Can you put it in your apartment until I get out of practice?"

Normally I would have told him to go shove his sarcasm up his tail, but the mere thought of Savoy coming and getting a chance to talk to her alone intrigued me. It'd been a little over a week since our kiss; I had given her space on purpose, to give her a chance to think things over. Maybe now it was put up or shut up. Since our time together, I had been with my ex and confirmed that she meant nothing to me and had a girl come on pretty strong that didn't know me at all and didn't become affected by her beauty. Savoy had a place in my heart and I needed to decide if I was going to let her understand that. Our place was a pigsty and it wasn't because I wasn't doing my part. My room was clean but the common area looked a mess. Four guys without a maid or mother to come behind us, we were going to have to do better and I couldn't blame anyone. I didn't want Savoy to come in and be turned off so I tidied up and thought, "Why should I tell her everything?" "Gotta keep her off balance," one side of me said. "Off balance—that's a joke. If you learned anything, Perry, it should be that girls love the vulnerable you. Tell her how you really feel. Only then will you have a real shot at her heart."

After cleaning, I must have dozed off. There was a soft knock on the door and I heard Savoy's voice say, "Perry, are you in there?"

I came out of my room and tripped on the end table. She must have heard me stumble. "Perry, you okay?"

"Yeah, yeah, I just fell."

I limped to the door and opened it.

"You sure you alright?" she said, helping me to the couch.

"My knee's still sore, man." At this point we were arm in arm, and as cute as Tori was and as hot as Anna looked, Savoy was beautiful to me. She had everything I wanted my woman to have, including beautiful naturally curly hair and hips that I could clearly see with the brief track shorts she had on.

"I need some water," I said as I wanted to put her on a plate and sop her up like gravy. "So you got your brother's stuff?" I said, pouring water into a glass, "Can I get you something to drink? Was your trip okay here?" I didn't even realize that I was seeming nervous, but I was. This girl definitely had me.

"Yes, I have my brother's stuff. No, I wouldn't like anything to drink, and the trip was cool. The question is: Are you feeling okay? I've never seen you so rattled. You've always been the cool, calm, and collected Perry Skky Jr. What's going on?"

The moment of truth was here. Did I dance around the issue or did I come straight at her with my feelings?

"Wow, I'm amazed on how clean your place is," she said to me, bailing me out of the subject.

"Oh yeah, we try to pick up around here. Our moms taught us well."

"Are you doing any workout on your leg? Lance told me you hurt it pretty bad. And you just tripped coming into the door like that. I was going to invite you to work out with me, but maybe you need to rest."

"Oh naw, putting a little pressure on it during a small jog will be good. Hold on. Let me get my stuff." Savoy was not only intelligent but athletic as well, and it certainly turned me on to watch her speed around me as I jogged. Running on her track was so private I loved it. It was completely different from the football field with reporters, coaches, and other teammates jockeying for attention. Since the track girls were training at different times, we had the place all to ourselves, and as Savoy passed me, I grabbed her hand.

"Hey, you need a break," I said to her, proud of her stamina.

"Not yet, I got three more laps around. Let me go."

I didn't want to let go of her hand, though. There was so much I needed to tell her, so much I needed to know, but she looked in my eyes waiting on me to say something, and I couldn't say it so I let her hand loose and she started running again. "What a chump you are," a side of me said. "She was right there looking square in your eyes. Why couldn't you tell her what you think?" But another side said, "Naw, you did the right thing, boy. Never let them floozies know what you thinking. Keep them guessing. Make her fall back in love with you without telling her that you're in love with her." I went over and got my water bottle and poured it all over my head, wanting to drown out both voices.

"I'm a head to the locker room. It was good working out with you."

"You going back now?" I asked, not wanting our time together to end.

"No, I'm thinking about going to Varsity and getting one of those big ol' chili slaw dogs and orange crème sodas and I'll hit the road home. What are you up to?" she asked. Her style was really cool, she wasn't trying to force anything on me, and I didn't want to invite myself where I wasn't welcome.

So I said, "I gotta appetite, that's cool?"

"Definitely, you want me to pick you up in front of y'all locker room in about thirty minutes?"

"Cool," I said to her.

I had forgotten that I was supposed to be recuperating. When I got into the locker room, Saxon asked all about his stuff.

"My sister's back on the road, right?"

Lance was right behind him. I didn't want them to know that I was hooking up with her in just a second. I looked all around, then Deuce came up behind me and said, "Dang,

y'all all on the man. Sax, I know your stuff is where it's supposed to be. You the boy trying to get ready for training
camp. Can he hit the showers?"

"I just want to know if she asked about me?" Lance got in
my face and said.

Boy, didn't I want to rub it in his face that she talked about
everything but him; however, I thought it best that I just leave
it alone. Why brag? In reality, Savoy and I were like me and
Tori and me and Anna—friends. When I went to the showers,
Deuce got me right before.

"I'm sure you gon' see Savoy again, huh?"

"How'd you know to have my back like that, man?"

"I could tell you were dodging the question. Brothers
dodge when they have something to hide. Y'all working it
out?"

"I don't know, man."

"Just enjoy her, she worked you out."

"We were at the track, fool," I said, messing with my friend.

An hour later I was staring into Savoy's eyes as she looked
so cute chomping on the loaded hot dog. Everyone had told
me that the Varsity was the spot I had to try. Supposedly it
had been a fixture around Tech's campus for years. And as
good as the food tasted, I could see why it was so special to
many fans.

"Seems like you've been wanting to tell me something all
day," Savoy said as she wiped the chili from her mouth.

No more evading the issue. If I wanted something real
with her, I was going to have to step up; be cool about my response but not let her think that she didn't matter.

"Last time we were together, I think something special
happened between us, I got to admit, I'd like more of that
but I don't want to push you."

"Perry, you really hurt me before but that kiss meant
something to me, too. I appreciate you giving me space these

last couple of days to just think. My brother told me that I need to give the stuff to you. I wanted to leave it on the front porch or mail it but a stronger part of me wanted to see you again, to see if what I felt that night was real. And just hanging out with you, laughing with you, running with you, enjoying time with you, I don't know, it just feels good. Do we have to know if we will have anything? Can we build on our friendship without me having to worry about you entertaining others 'til we figure this thing out?"

I wanted to tell her I'd been with others since I'd last been with her and they didn't move me; I just took her hand stained with chili and kissed it.

"We'll try it your way, slow. Okay?"

"Cool, I won't be back for a couple of weeks. Maybe after that we can go out or something. Maybe we can come here again. I'll be craving one of these hot dogs."

"I know, right," I joked.

"But I'll let you in on a little secret."

"What's that?" I said as she wiped chili from her mouth.

"I really like this nonpushy Perry. It's attractive."

~ 12 ~

Pampering Only Gold

"The real ballers are in the house!" a loud dark-skinned brother came into the locker room and said.

It was August 1, training camp was about to begin, and I truly hated that my leg wasn't ready for me to practice with the rest of the team. But getting to know the players from the sideline might prove itself to be very valuable. After all, being able start for the Yellow Jackets wouldn't be a popularity contest. It would be skill. Those that showed the coaches the most would be suited up the most, and I wanted to be a part of that number. The odds were against a freshman, and although the eighteen of us had worked hard, those that were here before us were back to claim their territory.

"I'm Lenard Pope, that's right. That's right," the loud-mouth guy continued. "The starting wide receiver and my boy here, Mack Brown, will be the other one on the other side. I hear it's two freshmen trying to take our jobs but one of you are hurt so I ain't worried about you. The other, where you at, man? Show your face if you ain't a punk."

I didn't know where Saxon was but this Lenard Pope guy was talking his language.

"Come on, man," Saxon came up behind me and said really

loudly, "Let's let this dude who's been here and ain't done nothing know that he can't fade us."

Lenard started walking toward Saxon and the crowd of football players gathered around. I didn't like the fact that Saxon was egging this guy on but he had a point. I knew nothing about Mack or Lenard because they were seniors and I had never gotten a lick of playing time. Saxon and I were recruited by two head coaches, the coach that got fired and Coach Red that replaced him. Both of them wanted us to stay because they didn't think the wide receivers they had on roster were good enough to win any games in the ACC.

"Hey, man," I said to Sax, "they think they all that, that's cool. You don't have to talk it up to prove it out there on the field. They're right, I'm hurt, I'm no threat, but you can hold your own out there."

For the first time in a long time, Saxon and I connected. He nodded in approval of my suggestion, and as he turned to walk away, I had Lenard and Mack in my face.

"So you're the Perry Skky Jr. I'm really supposed to be all worried about?"

"Naw, man, you don't have to worry about me. It's your thing."

Mack stepped in and said, "Yeah, it is our thing. Coach is about to hand out jerseys. First string gets gold, the other scrubs get blue."

"Y'all should know y'all on the sideline for the past three, four, five, six, seven years," Sax joked.

"Ooh, you better be glad you walked away, and who is he over there laughing with?" this white guy came up to Lenard and said.

The two of them acted like they were best friends. "Mario, now we got a quarterback, let's play ball."

Mario had on a gold jersey. I looked over at Lance and he

seemed so disappointed. Deuce went over to Lance as the upperclassmen cleared out.

"I can't let my boy stay down like this," Deuce said.

It was weird. Before the upperclassmen came in, we had our own rivalry thing going on between the freshmen, but now we had to stick together. They were too cocky for us not to knock them down. Deuce said to Lance as he placed his hand on his shoulder, "Man, Coach just gave me a blue jersey."

"Yeah, but I'm sure you won't be in yours long," he said. "Look, like coach favoring the color in the quarterback position. Must think a white boy can't throw."

I was all confused. I had just seen Mario, and he looked white to me. What the heck was Lance talking about?

"He's mixed, man," Saxon said to me as he saw the perplexed look I had posted on my face.

"All right, well, somebody talk to me."

"I'm sure it's nothing like that," Deuce said.

"Coach Red, his nickname is Red Neck!" Deuce was giving information I had never heard before. I certainly wouldn't have signed up to play with a guy that I thought had a problem with African-Americans.

"That's not true," Lance said.

I took my towel and popped Deuce in the back.

"Boy."

"I'm trying to cheer him up, dang. We just gone have to go out there and take our jobs. Coach want us to work for it, prove ourselves we can do that. Lance, Mario tries to sabotage. He don't throw the balls right to me. Work it out. Do it like we been doing it for the last three weeks. Let's show 'em both up. You down?" Both of them came to an agreement.

Their theory sounded really good, but when we got out in practice the next couple of days, the gold jersey players got way more reps than the blue.

"This ain't fair, Perry," Saxon came over to me and said during a break. "Least you not able to showcase your skills because you're injured. He won't even put me on the field to see what I can do. Dang, I should have gone to Clemson."

"Saxon Lee," Coach Red yelled from the other side of the field, "pick up that daggum helmet, boy. I don't know how they tolerated your poor attitude on your South Carolina high school team, but this is the big leagues, son. Give me fifty suicides."

"I hate it here," Saxon said as he began to oblige the coach.

"Hey, man, don't let him get you," I yelled out.

Mario, Lenard, and Mack were all average to me. I couldn't wait to get out on the field and catch Lance's passes. He clearly had a better arm, and although he wasn't getting as much practice as the current first-string quarterback, he was showing him up. The third day of practice most of the blue team was dragging. Coach didn't have the gold team doing as much warm-up work as the others. It seemed unfair to me, but I wasn't a coach. I was only used to everyone doing the same amount of conditioning. Tempers were high with my freshmen class, and when we hit the showers, Lenard came up to Saxon and said, "A few days ago you said to me all I needed was to see you out there on the field or was that your partner who pumped you up like that, that boy that's hurt. He can't even get out there and show us anything."

"What's your point?" Saxon said to him.

"My point is what I've seen you do is crap. You might as well get used to the idea of being red-shirted. After a year of watching me shine, maybe then you'll be ready." Saxon pushed him back.

"Come on, man, it ain't worth it," I said to Saxon.

"Listen to crip," Lenard joked.

"Who you calling crip?" Deuce said. "Your skills are the

ones looking handicapped. I'm catching more out of the backfield than you, and I'm a running back."

"Well, maybe it's not his fault," Lance jumped in and said. "Back to his poor pitiful quarterback, he can't even throw a straight arrow; couldn't put it in his hands if he were two feet away."

The way the four of us rallied together was something, though Saxon and Lenard went their separate ways. We were even apart in the cafeteria, gold team on one side and blue on the other. But later on that night before curfew, we had a meeting in my common room and all the freshmen put their two cents in on how they hated to be treated like stepchildren. I finally said, "Listen, guys, I've been watching all of you. I wish I could be running drills, at least one rep much less ten. I understand y'all are frustrated and want to show what you got, you really want to be able to compete for the starting job, but we're in college now. It's a new level; we can't let the coaches, upperclassmen, and anybody else make us feel like we don't deserve to be here. I've been with you guys for the last three weeks and nothing has been able to bring us close like these last few days have. We are a talented group, the paper says so, college analysis says so, and even Coach Red said so. So what if he wants to work us a little hard and not make us feel like prima donnas? Cool, we got each other, a'ight?" I said, wanting all of them to use their energy the right way.

They all clapped and cheered. We were all a cohesive group of freshmen ready to withstand the hard work so in the end we'd have the satisfaction of taking away those starting jobs.

"Perry, didn't you just buy some groceries for this house?" Collin came in and asked.

"Yeah, we were out of the basics, so I picked up milk, orange juice, some sandwich meat, wheat bread, and some fruit;

oh yeah, cereal. I love having Frosted Flakes as a late-night snack. What you want to have some of it, it's cool."

"No, that's not my problem. I mean, I bought some things a few days before you did and you bought stuff because everything was gone and I'm just wondering what our roommates are contributing into this equation. I mean, there's nothing in there now."

"What you mean, there's nothing in there now?"

"Go look."

I got out of my bed and went to the kitchen, went through the cabinets and the refrigerator, and I couldn't believe they were bare. Then I looked in the trash can and it was overflowing with empty cartons and boxes. I hadn't even had a drop of the orange juice I'd bought so I wondered where it went.

"You know when you first came and we all moved in here together and you bought groceries that day and everybody went through it, you know that was one thing," Collin said as his face turned red, "but my parents have only a little dough. They gave me a credit card but I have a limit. I can't keep buying groceries. My mom is gon' think I'm feeding the whole team. It's four of us in this place, but if it's not you buying it, then it's me. Seriously, when are the other two going to contribute? You need to talk to them about this," he said as he folded his arms and leaned against the countertop.

I closed the refrigerator door and had to admit that I was a little disappointed. I wanted a snack at ten thirty in the evening, but there was nothing.

"Why do I have to be the one that says something? You brought it to my attention. Just talk to 'em. I'm sure they'll buy something."

"So you're not mad?" he asked me. "You were hot before?"

"Yeah, I mean, and that's not right, shoot, we all live here and I'm not trying to label my food. I just had a problem with

Lance and I took it a little over the top. But I bring something in here . . . We got to take care of each other, right? That shouldn't be one-sided, and it looks like we're taking care of them and shoot my bank account can't handle it."

Lance came in between us and put his empty cereal bowl in the sink. He didn't rinse out the milk, he didn't put the bowl in the dishwasher, he didn't even put the plastic spoon in the trash. Collin flicked up his hand like "See?" Lance didn't owe me a thank-you for the food, but he did seem a little unconcerned that there was nothing left for the person that brought the groceries into the place to eat.

"Hey, man, can I talk to you for a sec?"

"Naw, partner, I'm on the phone with a chick," he flicked his hand at me and said.

"Wait a minute. You better go in there and tell her you'll call her back, or well, I'm sure she'll hold on because I know you got it like that. I'm hungry, man."

Lance rolled his eyes. Deuce came into the kitchen behind him.

"What are we doing, having a meeting and nobody told me?" he teased.

"Naw, he's telling me he's hungry. I don't know why he won't just fix himself some cereal like I just had. It was good."

"Oh, he can't eat that. I just got the last bowl full."

"I brought some sandwich meat and some fruit and none of that's in there y'all. Collin said he didn't eat any of it. I haven't had a drop of it."

"I thought we were trying to be like brothers, what's yours is mine."

"Yeah, but that's the problem, Lance. When is what's yours going to be ours? Perry and I are the only two who have brought something for this place."

"I'm not trying to start a big commotion about that. We

went through that when we moved in. Yeah, I don't mind sharing, but couldn't y'all have left me a little corner or something?"

"Better yet," Collin said, "when are y'all going to buy some groceries? Because I am high and tired of buying food I don't get a chance to taste."

"Do you believe this!" Lance said to Deuce.

"I thought you had gotten something to eat," Deuce said. "I heard somebody rambling in the kitchen before I even came in here. It must have been Lance but I thought it was you, so once you got something to eat, I was squared to go get something for myself. I'm sorry, man, but I don't have no dollars to replace it. My parents ain't got it like that."

"My dad is just a preacher with four kids," Lance said. "The only reason that I'm at Tech is because I got a scholarship."

"Well, then we got a problem," Collin said.

Collin looked at me like I could solve the dilemma. What were we supposed to do—make the two of them get cash from the sky?

"If they ain't got it, they ain't got it," I looked over at Collin and said.

"Maybe y'all need to talk to Coach about getting a job or something."

"How we gone get a job in the middle of training camp?"

"Well, they have snacks and things like that," I channeled in and said. "So instead of coming upstairs and grabbing what's in the refrigerator, you can grab what the university puts out."

Lance said, "So y'all can bring it into our house but we're not supposed to take any of it?"

For a man who didn't have a pot to piss in, I didn't know why that sounded so outrageous and ridiculous to him.

"Lance, dude, I was willing to share, but you cleaned me out of everything and you can't even replace it."

"You want me to walk down to the athletic dorm, Mr. Prima Donnas, and get you something to eat?"

"No, Lance, that's what you should have done for yourself!" Collin said as if I was incapable of setting his tail straight.

Being hurt did make me a little humbler. I had been a little nicer to everyone, but I wasn't losing my edge. Deuce at least seemed to understand where Collin and I were coming from, but Lance just thought he deserved a free ride when it was hard for all of us to try and make it.

"Perry, I mean seriously, my sister's told me about y'all's house and your dad's dealership, and you got a brand-new car sitting right around the corner. I don't even have a car at all."

"Yeah, man, but isn't that because you wrecked it?" Deuce channeled in.

Lance gave him a look like "you're supposed to be on my side."

"I'm just saying, Lance, we can't be mad at them, because of our situation."

"But if my parents had it going on like Perry's and, Collin, yours, too . . ."

"Lance, you don't even know anything about my family."

"I know your dad is some airplane pilot for Southwest, high up with seniority and stuff. I met him when he brought you to school. He was bragging. I'm just saying if my dad had it going on like the two of you guys, I wouldn't be sweating my roommates when my parents can barely bring bread into the crib."

I was so sick and tired of the segregation. If it wasn't a race issue or a first sting–second string thing, then it had to do with dollars. I considered myself a private person. My family's business was just that—our business. No one needed to know it. But it was like Lance was thinking we were the Trumps and it just wasn't that way. If I was to really grow closer to them, they needed to understand that my life wasn't so perfect.

Before I could speak, Collin said, "Look, my father does have seniority, but the airplane pilots are dealing with the airlines right now and who knows how that whole thing is going to turn out? He's got me on a budget."

"Alright fine, then, I'm sorry, Collin," Lance said. "But Perry, you can front us until the season starts and we get our little stipends from the university."

"You can't put the man on the spot like that," Deuce said to Lance.

"You were just saying what a stand-up guy he is. He seems selfish to me."

"Aren't you the pot calling the kettle black?" I said to Lance. "You just expect me to take care of you without even saying 'thank you.' I'm not asking you for any gratitude, but I also didn't ask you to eat up all the food as if no one else in here deserved to have some of the ham sandwich."

"You can go buy some more ham tomorrow, Perry. Aren't you hearing what I'm saying? Your dad is loaded. Share some of the wealth."

"All right news flash, big mouth," I said as I went over and took Lance's collar and turned it. "My father is being pressured by the corporation to sell his dealership. The dealership he's had in our family for years because my grandfather started it. My father doesn't even know how he's going to put food in my mom's mouth, much less y'all's. If I got it, you can have it, but don't go assuming things about my family when you really don't know what's going on."

I pushed him back a bit before I let him go. Being rich had its privileges, but I had to face facts. I couldn't live frivolously like I had before. I had to play by a new set of rules. Deuce came up to me before I opened my door and said, "Hey, man, we're sorry. We shouldn't have took advantage like that and I'm sorry about what's going on with your family. I pray it all works out."

Deuce and I were from opposite sides of the track, but at that moment when he mentioned praying for my family, we were brothers united in Christ. That filled me more than any piece of fruit ever could.

The whole team was excited. It was the first day of scrimmage—gold against blue—and though my knee felt better, Coach wanted me to have one more week off before practicing. Before the scrimmage, the coach separated the teams by color. When he came out from talking to the gold team, we heard cheers, chants, and screams. Saxon and Lance made it clear they detested being on the blue squad, and though they'd shown a few dynamic things, in reality they hadn't won the starting jobs outright. However, today was the day to change all of that. It wasn't about the reps; it was about making plays. When Coach Red came and talked to the blue team, he said, "I know some of you hate the fact that you are not first stringers. I've purposely taken care of the gold team so you could feel really small wearing blue jerseys, so small that you want that first-class treatment and would step up your game so that I would elevate you to the gold team. Ironically enough, only one of you over the past couple of weeks has impressed me enough to receive that honor." Lance and Saxon started smiling. Their arrogance was surreal; they were good but they weren't great. Coach Red continued, "And the young man that is stepping up to first string is so humbled, he's a hard worker. Even when he makes a great play, he's ready to make a better one the next go-round. He doesn't complain about how few reps he gets; he just makes the best of what he has. He tries to encourage and motivate those around him, a real selfless guy. Deuce Jones, step forward."

Lance and Saxon looked stunned. I started clapping and the rest of the blue team joined in. Finally the two of them got on board. Deuce deserved it. He was everything Coach said and more. His room was right beside mine. I heard him doing push-ups in the middle of the night. We both prayed together that God would give him favor and heal my leg. He was the first freshman to join the upperclassmen, when Coach made him take off the blue jersey and put on the gold one. I screamed, "Yeah!"

Coach gave the blue team a few more words about what he expected from the performance in the scrimmage. When he gave everyone a second to compose themselves after running out into the field, I walked into Sax and Lance pouting.

"This is good and all," Saxon said, "but he ain't the only one that deserves a gold jersey."

"Yeah, Coach is tripping."

"Come on, y'all, don't hate," I said to them. "Deuce ain't even gonna be able to enjoy this if he see y'all bitter. Be a real friend. Least you get to play today. Look at me. I got to sit on the sideline. I should be the one complaining."

"A'ight, a'ight. I hear you," Saxon said to me.

Lance didn't acknowledge that he got me at all; however, his actions spoke louder than any of his words could speak to me. He walked straight up to Deuce and I saw them exchange grips. Everyone cleared out but Deuce was dragging his feet as he tied his cleats.

"You better hurry up and get out there, boy," I said to my friend. "You got to meet your other team members. Go, man." I posed like the Heisman trophy.

"Boy, stop," he said. "You'll be a first string as soon as you get healthy, and you know it. Lenard and Mac are going to have to sit back."

"That may be, man, but not today. I'll be cheering for you, buddy."

"Can I tell you something, Perry?" Deuce asked as I put one shoulder pad under his jersey.

"Yeah, sure, you can talk to me about anything."

"I prayed for this opportunity and I'm excited that it's here, but dang, man, what if I get out there and embarrass myself on the first play—drop a pass or something? I was excited about easing into this role and now I'm the first one the coach just threw on the gold team. All eyes are going to be on me. I don't know if I'm ready."

"Uh-unh, boy, you ain't gon' be doubting yourself like that. That's the devil trying to get you all down. Making you think you can't when all you need is the strength to persevere through the uncertainty, and so what if you get shaken up on a play or two? It's not gon' do nothing in the big scheme of things. Coach wouldn't put you on gold team if he didn't think you could be there. I also know that you're ready, and deep down"—I pointed at his chest—"you know you're ready, too. Now get the heck out there and show the rest of them you came here to play."

"You're right," he said as he started gaining confidence. "Not here to show boat, not here to show out, I just came to show up and do my part."

"That's right." We clasped hands and then hugged.

Any other day I would have been like Saxon and Lance, a little disappointed that I wasn't the first man that was in a gold uniform from our freshman class, but God was doing something greater in me than just having me here to play football. He was growing me as a man, growing me as His child. I could feel myself growing closer to His glory as I walked away more and more of my own selfishness. As I encouraged Deuce, I encouraged myself, too. I wasn't out there this week, but I would be out there next week, and my goal was to be playing in a gold uniform, and unless the Lord said different, I was sure to have given it all that I could to come back and shine.

When I went out to the field, I was a little disappointed that the Tech fans didn't show up in large numbers. It was interesting to me that as I listened to the hype in shows and read write-ups, the fans were the first to criticize what they thought the team needed to do, but when it came time to show up on game day or even fan day, they were absent. What the heck was that about, requiring more from your team than you're willing to give? If this were Auburn or Georgia or Clemson or Virginia Tech, the first scrimmage going into the season would be packed. Deuce's first play from scrimmage fumbled. I could hear Lenard yell, "You might be catching more passes than me out the backfield, freshman, but you can't hold on to the ball when it's placed right into your hand."

"That's alright, that's alright," Coach said, encouraging Deuce. I thought that same thing in my mind, hoping that my friend could connect and understand what I told him in the locker room. So what if the first play or two got discombobulated? Settle in, focus, and tote the mail. And when the coach put it in his hands the second time, that was exactly what he did and ran sixty-two yards. The few fans that were there roared. From then on, though it was a defensive battle, first-string defense and second-string defense were whooping up on the offense, no score was to be had, but I could've covered my ears hearing all the guys cuss. For real, man, I wasn't a saint, but dang, I hadn't been around the defensive guys much, but every other word, if not every word, was something foul. And it wasn't just me. I heard a little boy in the stands say to his mom, "Aren't they saying things that you told us not to say?"

Then an alumnus looked over at them and said, "Yeah, son, but as long as those guys tote the mail for us and win some ball games, we don't care what they say. They're really not here to get an education." I was appalled.

Then another alumnus said, "No, we want them to graduate. That helps with recruiting. Football's a rough sport so we do overlook the bad language."

Coach Red must have heard the comments from the stands because he turned around and eyed the fans when the scrimmage was over. As we headed into the locker room, the defense were chanting and cheering as if they'd won a national championship. Coach Red yelled, "Everybody to the center of the floor now!"

Our offense got creamed. What was he going to say to the defense? Did they do a good job?

Finally, when we were all together, he stood in the middle of the circle as some guys kneeled. "Listen, today I lost respect for you as a team. If your mothers and fathers were out there and could have heard your foul language, knowing your great parents as I do, all of you would be getting reprimanded. Your folks raised you better than that, and even if they give you a little leeway, I'm not going to have trash talking on my team. There were people in the stands that were talking about how pitiful and disgusting your mouths were. We're wondering why this place isn't packed. It just might be because no one wants to be around your disgusting tails, and defense, I'm extremely disappointed in you. You act like you won out this game and you beat out your offense. We play Notre Dame at the beginning of the season and do you think they're rooting and raving like that when they make the offense look like wimps? This is a team sport. You need to be encouraging the offense to get their asses together so that we don't get killed soon, and offense, just so you know—from now on, everybody has a blue shirt. All positions are up for grabs. You all look pitiful, and it's my fault because I've been pampering only the gold players."

"They're not here . . ."

"So are you going to let me in on why you messing with me like this?"

"Nah, I just wanted us to talk in the morning."

"Boy, you are silly," I said.

And then I walked into my room. My eyes did a double take when I saw a brunette in my bed in a swimming suit—a bikini no less—and it look like whatever size she was wearing was too small.

"I thought you'd never get here, Perry," the girl said as if she knew me.

I just stood still, frozen at the door as if an angel were holding me back. This couldn't be happening. I just prayed about temptation, and not even five minutes later, I'm faced with a big one.

"I'm not going to bite," she said, "and my top is actually hurting." She leaned up and took her arms toward her back as if she was actually about to let the button loose.

"I heard you about to go on the field tomorrow, and I'm just here to give you a little present."

"Excuse me just for a second," I said as I held my finger up.

Quickly, I went back out into the family room area. The TV was off and there was no sight of Lance. I couldn't believe his white behind jetted. He was the only one home. No wonder he was looking so coy. He'd probably set the whole thing up. Well, it was not funny. I didn't even knock on his door. I just turned the knob and it was unlocked.

"Wassup, what's the meaning of this?" I said to him.

"You tell me, partner. She came to the door and said you told her to wait. Does this sound like something I would do? I don't know you that well. She was hot. She said she was going to rub you down and get you ready to play tomorrow,

~ 13 ~

Speaking Problems Away

"Thank you, Lord, for blessing me. Just getting cleared by the team trainer to go out tomorrow and compete, I'm feeling good, and I know that I can only give you the glory for that," I said as I entered my apartment. "It hasn't been easy to stand on the sidelines, but I hope I've made you proud encouraging others. Keeping the green-eyed monster in check, I pray I continue to stay focused on you. College is a crazy world. You never know what temptation is lying around the corner. But by confessing I'm not perfect, I know you can help me stay focused in Jesus' name, Amen."

When I entered the apartment, Lance was sitting on the couch watching TV. He got up out of his seat and teased, "Dang, I wanna be like you when I grow up. You are the man."

I really did have a pretty quick recovery, I just assumed that, but he was looking so smug like I was mischievous or into something bad and I didn't understand what that was all about so I asked, "Okay, what's the joke? Why are you trying to say I'm the man?"

"Don't act like you don't know."

"Where are Deuce and Collin, they're around the corner? I'm on *Candid Camera*, what's going on?"

and you knew all about it. That's why I said, 'You're the man.' I thought you were teasing me not knowing what I was talking about, but I guess all this was a surprise. Don't be mad at me. But if you want me to take her off your hands and all . . ."

"Lance, I don't want Savoy to hear a word about any of this. I know you still like her and about six other girls."

"I didn't want to say nothing, God. Seriously, I know you got real feelings for the chick. You even growing on Saxon."

"What you mean?"

"I mean, don't worry about it. You got a hot chick over cross the other side of dis place . . . for real for real you don't go over there and handle your business I'm a go over there. You think she's a Tech student? Yeah, but she looks like an upperclassman. She way too filled out to be a scrub."

Lance drew the outline of a curve-shaped body with his index fingers. He came to his door and I pushed him back in it and went outside and closed it. If he wasn't the culprit that had set this whole thing up, I needed to talk this girl and get to the bottom of the mystery.

When I got back to my room, I was surprised to find the girl under my covers, and from what I could see, there were no straps on her shoulders.

"Hey, listen," I said.

"I don't wanna get out this bed 'cause it feels all comfy, but if you don't come join me by the count of three, I'm going to be forced to come over there and pull you in although it's nighttime, it's ninety degrees, and you guys don't even have the A/C on. I'm burning up. You got to want to get out of those clothes."

She stuck out her tongue and licked her finger slowly. The last thing I needed was to get off-focus. Although Savoy wasn't coming back to Tech for another week or two, I was committed to trying to make things right, and she might never know if I went ahead and obliged what a part of me wanted to undertake. But my soul wouldn't be able to rest.

"Look, I don't even know your name."

"I'm Chastine, Lenard's girlfriend." I almost choked. "Do you need some water or something? I can get up and get it for you."

"No, no, no. You stay put. Lenard's girlfriend? I'm already not his favorite person; he'd freak if he knew you was here."

"He and I had a bet and he lost."

"What does that have to do with me?"

"He had to grant me my fantasy and that was having fun with one of the freshmen. And you definitely were the one I wanted to tear about, so this is his gift to you."

I couldn't believe his girl was serious. What kind of relationship did Lenard have with his girl? She thought it was cool to be shared by everyone on the team. And although she didn't tell me I wasn't the first, I got the feeling this was a common practice between the two of them.

"So do you go to Tech?"

"Oh no, I'm not in school."

I hated to say that made sense to me, but no intelligent girl would think the situation was okay. She came in my room to get busy, but I needed to tell her some serious business.

"Chastine, don't take this the wrong way 'cause you're a gorgeous girl. First of all, I have respect for people's relationships."

"It's cool with him, really. I've been dreaming about you. From what I've seen of your body on TV, they can't even compare, right?"

"I'm flattered seriously, but I mean, he's my teammate."

"You're not scared, are you?"

"No, I've just asked for trouble sometimes with the bad choices I make."

"What do you mean? This is just me and you. Who sees?"

I took my hand and pointed at the ceiling. My room was small, but she knew I wasn't talking about the light above us.

"I knew you were a good guy and all, but I didn't know you like believed in God."

"Yeah, I do, and I really feel like I'm supposed to be telling you, you have way more going for you than just offering up your body to strangers."

"Perry, Lenard met me at the strip club. Trust me, I'm so far gone, if there is a God, he forgot about me many moons ago."

"Well, that's just the thing. See, God is in the forgiving business, and I'm not one to judge, but the one who can doesn't forget about you."

"I don't know if I'm ready for all that yet."

"I'm not here to push what I believe on you, but you gotta respect the way I'm trying to live, you know."

"Something to think about," she said.

I walked out of the room and gave her a chance to dress. About two minutes later she came out in daisy dukes and a bathing suit top intact. I stood at the front door and held it open.

"Chastine, I really hope you think about what I said. You're too special for this."

She pulled my neck toward her and planted a kiss on my lips.

"Thanks for the advice and for something I'll treasure."

At that moment it would be horrible timing for me that Deuce and Collin came home.

"Don't even ask," I said to them as I shut the door.

* * *

I was supposed to be concentrating on going out on the field and practicing drills, trying to get ready to be on the gold team. But Lenard came up in my face and said, "So what you are going to insult me by not accepting my gift, freshman?" And he pushed me back.

"Don't even come to me with that junk."

"You're telling her I don't care, because I let her have a little fun. How you going to try and wreck what I got?"

"You need to be happy. I stepped away 'cause if I got with her, she wouldn't be coming back to you ever." The few people that was around us said, *"Oooooooo!!!"*

"She told me you couldn't perform. You call it being a Christian. I said maybe you a fag."

"Sticks and stones, Lenard. You still in kindergarten, man? Like I give a crap what you think about me. I'm not hurt no more, so let's take it to the field."

"Yeah, let's take it to the field."

I wasn't threatening him, but I was confident in my ability. After all, I've always been able to let my ability shine. No way I couldn't be sticking my foot in my mouth this time, right?

Before I went out on the field, I rewrapped my knee. I guess I was getting a little nervous. Though we weren't wearing pads in practice and I didn't have to worry about someone hitting me in the wrong spot, I didn't want to plant my foot the wrong way either without the proper support. I didn't even realize I rewrapped my knee three times. I couldn't be wimpin' out. I had done this millions of times before—suited up and gone out on the field and jammed. But over the last eight months this injury had plagued me and maybe that was going to be too much for me to overcome. "You can't talk like that," the positive side of me said, but then of course, the doubter side in me responded by saying, "Same old knee hasn't gotten well yet. What makes you think it's well now?

As soon as you step out there, you're going to fail, you're not ready." "All you gotta do is remember that with God, all things are possible." "Knowing the scripture and believing the scripture are two totally different things," the negative side of me said. I sat back there in the locker room on the bench. My cell phone rang. I was already late for warm-ups, but it was like a sign. That call was supposed to uplift me somehow so I answered it.

"Perry, is that you?" the frail sad familiar voice said.

"Tori?" I questioned, wanting to kick myself for not looking at the caller ID before I answered the stupid phone.

"Yeah, it's me. Are you busy?"

"Well, I'm about to go to pra—you know what? You sound like you need to talk. What's up?"

"It's my mom!"

"What do you mean, it's your mom. What's going on?"

"She's undergoing surgery right now."

"What . . . what happened?"

"They think one of her ovaries might have cancer. The only way to find out is to do a biopsy."

"Are you at the hospital?"

"Yeah, but being in a waiting room with my dad and everybody is too much. I had to get away. I . . . I'm scared . . ."

"Well, look, I'm not trying to minimize this or anything, but a couple years ago my mom had a hysterectomy. Maybe that's all it is for your mom. They take everything out and she'll be good. No cancer, you know?"

"How am I supposed to breathe over the next couple hours? They say cancer is hereditary, and I don't want my mom to have it because I don't want to lose her, but I don't want her to have it 'cause I don't want her to lose me."

"Tori, don't jump the gun. You gotta think positive. God's got you. He's got your mom. You know you told me that many days when I was going through stuff with football and

I didn't start getting my mind right until I actually believed it. Can I pray for you?"

As I begin lifting up Tori's situation, one of the coaches screamed, "Skky, they've been looking for you and you're in here on the phone. Boy, get out there on that field."

"Oh, I'm getting you in trouble," Tori said.

"Just stay upbeat, okay? Your mom is going to be okay, but you gotta believe it."

When I hung up the phone, I grabbed my helmet and ran out on the field and didn't even think about not succeeding. God allowed us to go through the tough stuff for a reason. Never in a million years would I have wanted to get that call from Tori about her mom in surgery, but being able to encourage her, I was encouraging myself at the same time. Negativity leads to failure. The devil gets the victory and God can't do His job. Faith is the essence of things hoped for in the evidence of things not seen. I wanted to separate myself. Coach Red grabbed my neck.

"Listen, son, when practice is at five o'clock, you don't need to get your butt out here at five-oh-three. Do you understand?"

"Yes, sir, Coach."

"If I ever have to send a coach in looking for you, you might as well not bother coming in that day. Am I clear?"

"Yes, sir, Coach."

"Now how are you feeling? You ready to get out there and work that knee or do you think you still need to rest, 'cause if you're having second thoughts that we're pushing you too soon, then we don't need to rush this injury. 'Cause there are still a couple weeks before the first game."

"I'm ready to go, Coach. I was just rewrapping it. Sorry I was late."

"Nah, you weren't rewrapping your knee. You were on the cell phone. I already got the word, so let's be honest about what's going on here. You've always been labeled a good kid in my book, don't give me a reason to change my opinion of you."

"Yes, sir, Coach."

"Now hit the track and run a mile."

After running good, I took the field. My first three catches out of the back field were on point. I caught one from 20 yards out then 35 yards out then 52. But when defense lined up against me, I got two passes intercepted in a row. The first one I didn't run fast enough to get down the field and catch the ball. The second one I didn't jump high enough to break up the pass from the defender.

Coach yelled out, "Skky, your knee is the thing recovering, not your hands. Grab the ball before the DB can."

When we went back to the huddle, Lenard laughed.

"I mean, you've been waiting all that time for that? Come on, Pope, let's keep it together," Mario said, being the quarterback and team leader. "Let's keep the huddle free from personal attacks. I'm sick and tired of the defense thinking they own us. We got to start working like a team. Perry, catch the ball or deflect it away."

We went to line up again, and when the pass came to me, I dropped it. I was trying to keep the negative side of me from speaking but it was too hard. Coach took me out of the lineup and put Saxon in. I ended up watching from the sideline like I had done for the last couple of weeks. I could've kicked myself when I finally got a chance to showcase my skills; my will wasn't strong enough to fight through the nerve. When we walked into the locker room, Lenard came up behind me.

"So, we're not in the huddle now, freshman. Everywhere I go, I hear about Perry Skky Jr. You were just a high school phenomenon. Ain't nothing you can do up here on this level. And to think you tried to tell me you'd show me up. Looks like you got embarrassed, player. Wait—why am I calling you that? You not good with the ladies or on the field, busta."

My momma always told me if you have nothing good to say, then don't say nothing at all, because I knew if I responded to that chump, it wouldn't be verbally. My fist would be down his throat. I didn't even want to eat dinner with the team, so after I showered and changed and knew I didn't have to go to a team meeting, I decided to grab a sandwich and head up to the library to study for an upcoming exam. I had actually been breezing through the two summer courses I was taking. Studying for me was a good thing though I wasn't a whiz kid or anything like that, but in reality I probably needed to be on the field instead of in the library. Scholastically I might have challenges at Tech but at that moment I was cool. My cell phone rang and I hoped it was Tori giving me an update, but I looked at the caller ID this time and saw it was Cole.

"Hey, bud, tell me your day was better than mine," I said.

"Perry."

"Cole, man, what's wrong?"

"I broke my leg today, man. They going to red-shirt me. I'm going to miss the whole season."

"Awh, no, Cole. No, God, no!" I said, empathizing with my good buddy.

"I'm sorry I didn't call you more when you were injured 'cause it's like I got the plague around here. I'm in a whole different class now. I was like the most important freshman player until I hurt my leg today and now it's like nobody even knows I exist."

"Man, you can't think about that. You just got to take your time and heal and get well and be happy for the good education, 'cause this red shirt is great. You'll be able to come back next year and still have your four years of eligibility."

"But I want to be out there playing so bad. I was impressing everybody, my defensive line back coach said he had never seen a player work as hard as me. And on one play I cut to the left, everybody piles on top of my leg, and it breaks. I'm so depressed."

"Hey, man, this just happened. It's all right to give yourself time to be bummed out about it, but you can't stay down. I had a horrible practice today and I'm not telling you anything that I don't need to hear myself. Life will seem better tomorrow. Hold on."

The next day at practice was no different than the day before. I was favoring my knee and couldn't run full speed. Feeling the pain there, I hobbled all over the place, and because I kept thinking whether it would hold up or not, when passes came my way, I didn't catch them. But unlike the day before, Coach didn't take me out of the rotation even though I was wearing a blue jersey and not first string. Though my reps were few, they were consistent enough. Talk about confidence gone, I didn't feel healed physically or mentally. Apart from falling out and crying in front of everyone, I was a basket case in every other way that counted. I couldn't wait 'til practice was over so I could hit the shower up and head home, but I didn't get too far away without getting detained. This time it wasn't a jerk-off of a player; it was the chaplain.

"I know you're hungry, man, but I wanted to steal a bit of your time. Is that cool?" C. Moss said to me.

I had been at Tech for a month and I wouldn't say I was avoiding him or anything like that, but the incident at Hilton Head was so eerie, I just felt if I stayed away from his ministry, maybe I'd do better. As players began to leave the locker room to head up to eat, I got the same look from person after person, one that was like we're so sorry for you—superstar gone bust—and granted I never said I was the man. I never asked for all the media attention and don't recall me ever saying I wanted to take anyone's starting job. But because so many others said that for me and it appeared that it was not going to manifest itself, no one could hide their disappointment except maybe Lenard, because though he didn't say anything to me that day, he certainly was smiling from ear to ear, happy that his position was secure.

The chaplain's office was connected to the lounge area, and once everyone was gone out, it was just the two of us in this big ol' open space. We didn't even have to go into his quarters for privacy.

"I haven't wanted to intrude with you, Perry. I figured you and I had a rapport, and you knew where my office was so if you wanted to talk about your injury or what happened this summer or anything, you knew where I was. I honestly waited and waited for you to come so we could discuss stuff and I think I was tired of waiting. I needed to be proactive. I know it can be tough."

C. Moss had gone into the NFL and won the starting job after being drafted. In a later round he got injured and never got his big contract.

"I'm cool, Coach." Though he didn't coach a position, most of us called him coach anyway. In the program booklet he was chaplain/motivational coach, and boy, could he fire someone up. At that moment, though, I was the opposite of wanting to be restored. I felt broken beyond repair.

"I'm not going to pressure you, but we do have training camp service on Sunday. I think the message will inspire you."

"I'll see," I said as I got up and shook his hand before exiting.

Driving to Subway to get a club sandwich, I thought about Cole and what he had told me about being treated differ-

ently. When I was injured, I was still getting first-class treatment from everyone because I was supposed to come back
sharper, crisper, better, but because that wasn't happening
today, I could understand what that meant. I hated letting
people down and seeing it on their faces, and I had no idea
what I was going to do about it. Yeah, I'd keep working with
the trainers. Yeah, I'd keep going to practice and giving it my
all. But a part of me felt like doing all that wasn't going to do
any good. I was really a mess.

About 10 P.M. that night I was deep in sleep when I was
awakened by a knock at the door. At first I thought I was
dreaming, but when the bang became more persistent, I
said, "I'm tired, sleeping, check you in the morning."

"Hey, man, I need to talk to you for a sec."

"Serious, Deuce, I'm tired, man."

"He's not the only one who wants a bit of your time,"
Collin said.

"Guys, I'm fine."

"Man, let us talk to you for a second," Lance said.

"It's unlocked."

I pulled the covers over my head so they would get the
point that for real I was too tired to entertain, but Lance just
came over and pulled the bed clothes off me completely.

"Just a second, Perry, that's all. We just want to talk to you
for a second."

I sat up and put my head against the headboard.

"What's up?"

"A'ight, so you suck in practice. Everybody knows that."
Deuce hit Lance in the arm.

"Man, you ain't have to say it like that."

"I'm saying Perry's a big boy. Let's call a spade a spade. He
hadn't been doing well, everybody thinks he so great and he
looked horrible."

"Okay, and you came in here to cheer me up?"

"Well, that's the point. We know what we know, but we came in here to tell you that it doesn't have to be that way."

Collin said, "Perry, I think you have a mental block."

"What?" All three of us looked at him and said it together.

"You know it's when your mind makes you think you can't, you're under mind control, and you feel pains that aren't really there."

" 'Cause I am feeling some kind of pain. I'm not making it up, y'all."

"Right, but it's probably not in your knee."

Then Lance just took off the covers and hit me in my knee.

"Ooowah!"

"Boy, what are you doing?" Deuce asked him.

"That didn't really hurt, right?"

"Naw, it didn't hurt that bad," I said.

"Then maybe Collin has a point."

"Okay, Lance is crazy." Deuce pushed him back and said to me, "There's chapel tomorrow. You need to come. It's definitely been keeping me going. If this is all in your mind, you got to turn it over to God. Being all down on your abilities, telling yourself you're defeated—that's not you, man."

"Alright, y'all, I appreciate the pep talk," I said to my roommates.

The next morning was chapel. C. Moss had always been there for me and there was no way I wanted to let him down, but I just wasn't feeling the getting close to God right now and maybe that was where I was going wrong. Sitting in the room couldn't hurt much as I got dressed to head out to practice. I sat in the back of the room, which was packed. Guys I had heard using profanity were sitting up in chapel and I was definitely excited about that, but if they weren't being changed, could what I heard change me?

C. Moss started straight into his sermon by giving us the topic: "You Are Healthy and Whole."

"Today I want to talk to you guys from John 5, verses 8 and 9. The word says Jesus said to an invalid, 'Stand up, take your mat and walk.' At once the man was made well and he took up his mat and began to walk. You guys know that I believe in the power of positive thinking. Can I have a few shout-outs of what you think of yourself?"

Lenard stood up and said, "I'm great."

Everyone in the room started laughing, of course.

Mac stood up next and said, "I can. That's what I say when I'm on the field. I can."

"A'ight, a'ight," C. Moss replied. "Good."

Saxon stood next and said, "I will, I know I can. I get it done. I say I will."

"Okay, well, all of those are great responses, and I believe whatever you put inside, you put out. The word says, 'What a man thinketh so is he,' but sometimes it's not about what you think. It's about what you know, and if you studied this scripture here, there was a man that was lying there for years thinking that he could not get up, but Jesus came over to him and said, 'Look, you need to quit tripping. Get your tail up. Take up that daggum bed and walk out of here.' "

Everybody loved the way C. Moss explained the scripture. He wasn't your common preacher. He added a little flavor to it that had everyone, even the heathens, intrigued, but as I listened closely, he was saying something important, and I needed to make sure that I didn't miss the point in the midst of the fun way the message was being delivered.

"The guy had the ability to get up the whole time, I believe, but in his mind he bogged himself down thinking that he couldn't. It wasn't until Jesus told him he could that he knew he could. So I'm saying to all you guys, whatever your barrier is in life, whatever you think you can't do, know that Jesus is telling you, 'You're great, you can, you will,' get up and make it happen, and whatever the Lord says rules. Believe that you are more than a conqueror in Christ Jesus because you are healthy and whole and your body is a temple of healing life. If you know you're one with God, then and only then are you truly able to start speaking problems away."

~ 14 ~

Getting Great Encouragement

"That chapel was for you, you know?" C. Moss came up to me and said after he was done with the message. "I'm really glad you showed up."

I took my hand and put it on his shoulder, looked him straight in the eye, and said, "I'm glad I showed up, too."

"Sometimes God knows just what you need to get you through."

"That was right on time for me. Thanks."

When I took my hand off his shoulder, we still held eyes. It was like we could communicate without saying a word. I got every word he said, and I thought Jesus was speaking to me. I was already healed. All I needed to do was buy into it, believe it. Take up my insecurities and know that I'm healed. "I feel charged," I told him.

"My question is, how do you plan to stay energized, Perry? You'll have other bad practices. Believe it or not, you're not going to catch every pass. Does that mean you're not the man? Does that mean you will not fulfill your dreams and desires with the game of football? Naw, it just means you can't lose it when things get a little rocky. You've got to make sure that you do things that are going to uplift you. Be around folks that got your back, stay in God's word, you know what

I'm saying? And that's why I'm here on this campus. I care about X's and O's, but more than anything, I care about your soul."

"And the soul of every other player on this team. I hear you," I told Coach Moss. And I was finally getting it. My mind had been playing so many tricks on me the last three months, if not longer, probably because I had been through so much I was beating myself up thinking more negatively than positively about everything, and that was not healing for the mind.

"I want you to go and step out on that field and know that you know it is all good, Perry Skky, Jr. You're a child of the King."

That really sounded good. I was God's child. He wasn't going to let me fall. I had to receive that to truly know that and live every day believing that.

"You and I hadn't gone in deep about what happened this summer. I was waiting on you to come to me. I've said that before I didn't want to pressure you, and all that. But I just have it heavy on my heart to check on you where that's concerned because that's another part of healing. If you're bogged down with past drama, those pains and burdens you'd continue to carry will only pull you down."

"Well, thanks for giving me space, and honestly, I'm trying to get over it, and getting through it, I was starting to see everybody in the world as a different color and me as a racist and that's not what God wants. I've had a few other segregation issues; I'm trying to work through those now. You praying for me is helping me though."

"So don't stop."

"Cool, I won't."

An hour later I was on the field and catching passes that made me look and feel like Superman. I heard aws and ooohs from my teammates and from the coaches and the media that

were there. It was like I was back to my old form just believing it, just having my mind right, just knowing that my knee
could hold up. My vertical leap extended my reach and I
caught passes that should have gone over my head. Or my
jump extension allowed me to catch passes that were too
wide. The defenders couldn't stop me. No pass thrown my
way that day did I let them deflect.

"Yes, Lord!" I shouted, forgetting all those who were
around me and just putting all my concentration on me and
God. It was our time. It was our moment. He let me know
that I could. He didn't give up on me. He didn't leave me
feeling lost, and for that, I had to shout, not giving a care
who was around. To God be the glory in my life. That day He
was doing it.

"Dang, boy, you the man," my rival Mac came in and said
with his hand in the air, ready for me to give him a high five.

I should have been skeptical but I wasn't. We were a team.
Why shouldn't those who were once my foes be my friends?
If I looked better, my team would hopefully have a better
chance of winning. Everybody needed to step up, not just
me. So I appreciated it when Mario came up to me and said,
"Yeah, okay, so where you been hiding all that talent, dang."
The half-black dude was eloquent and cool. He, too, had
been standoffish but he, too, was embracing me.

"Hey, man, I know we gave you a hard time some this
summer, but that's what we need to see on Saturdays. I just
let on that you didn't have any skills but I read about you, I
watched your film. We were so happy when you decided to
sign with Tech and this is why. If I'm off my game a little too
high, a little too wide, even too low, I got a better chance
with you out there and Mac knows it. Welcome to first string,
baby."

"Naw, man, Coach ain't said nothing like that to me."

"I'm telling you," Mac commented on it. "He gon' give

you my job. And I can't be mad. I'm a senior, I want to play, and I know I'll get my time, but you got skills that got to be displayed. So look, we cool?"

"Man, I'm glad y'all were hard on me. I just didn't like letting you down at first when I was told I could come back and practice."

The three of us continued to lift one another. I couldn't just let them go on and on about me. They had been on this team for years, and even though we freshmen wanted to come in and rule, in order to be a great leader, you got to be able to be a great follower, too. Eating in the cafeteria didn't feel like I was on an island. Different players came up to me and said some positive things, and I appreciated every word, but I was still humble telling them I had way more work to do.

Everyone around me left when Coach Red came over and sat down. "So you showed up today, huh?" he said in his own way, letting me know he appreciated my performance.

"Sorry it took so long, Coach."

"I appreciate that, Skky. I know you work hard. I quite frankly was surprised when I knew what you were capable of, but you had to believe that you had it. You had to know you were great. And now I think you know that, I've heard you downplay it with the guys, and I like that class even more. You don't need to rub it in anybody's face. With outstanding talent, let that speak, not your mouth. I want you to come in a little early tomorrow and change your jersey out."

I knew what he was saying but I couldn't believe he was saying it. Mac told me it was going to happen but I couldn't believe what Coach Red was telling me. I was going to be on first string.

"What do you mean, Coach?" I said, trying to keep my cool.

"I got to get you a gold jersey. You think you gon' be able to handle that, son?"

"Oh, I won't let you down again."

"Yeah, you will. You're a college football player. Trust me, you'll let me down again, but I believe you'll make me proud more than you make me down. I am a Christian, son, and I have heard you in many different interviews giving God the glory for your athletic ability. He gives us different talents, but I do have to agree with you that you're something special. I've coached on the pro level and college for several years. You know I was offensive coach when we won the national championship, and I have never seen a player with as much talent and athletic ability as you."

"I appreciate that, Coach."

"Keep up the hard work. Keep on believing in yourself and stay on your knees, not dropping passes, of course."

We both chuckled.

"I'll stay connected with God."

"Congrats, son, for being Tech's starting receiver in the fall."

"Thank you, Coach." We both stood and shook firmly on it.

"You're going to take us to far places."

I could only smile and inwardly thank God.

I woke up the next morning and was truly excited. It was fan day and I was going to be represented as a starter for the Georgia Tech Yellow Jackets. It wasn't game day but it made it sort of feel like it. I had to tell myself, "You earned this, you deserved this, but dang boy, calm down."

Deuce was the only one in our house that was first string and actually the only freshman who had gotten the honors until yesterday when Coach gave me the news. I was a little nervous about how Sax and Lance would react. They'd been out there working hard doing everything the coach had asked, and in my opinion outshining Lenard and Mario, but the coach wasn't impressed enough to make the switch. I

only had one good day, but it was daggum sure a shining moment. Would they trip? Surely they would, knowing them.
Then there was a knock at my door.

"Hey, you got a sec? Can I come in?" I heard Deuce's voice
ask.

"Yeah, boy, come on, come on."

"Man, I had to get with the trainer the other day to work
on my shoulder. I had to take a couple of deep hits, but
what's up with you? You the man now, joining me on offense."

"Oh, so you heard?"

"Man, I've been praying that this would happen. You know
how hard it was to see you fumbling, wrestling around, acting
like you didn't know what you were doing. I watched film on
you, too. Remember we played y'all in the state game. I'm
glad you showed up." The two of us slapped hands.

"Anybody else heard?"

"Yeah, everybody knows."

I looked away, and he didn't offer what they were thinking, so I knew my gut feeling was correct.

"You ready to head over?"

"Naw, I need a little quiet time and go meet Coach first."

"That's right. Go get the jersey swapped out and everything."

As soon as he left, my cell phone started ringing. I looked
at the number and noticed it was Tori. I had completely forgotten the crisis she was in the last time we had spoken. Her
mom was going through a pretty significant surgery. Wrapped
up in my own life, I couldn't believe I hadn't followed up
with her.

"Hey, girl," I said, picking up the phone and feeling bad
about not responding.

"Hey, Perry," she said in a very excited way.

I guess I was surprised by that. It's not that I thought

she'd be mad at me for sure or that she was calling me to give me bad news about her mom but I wasn't expecting Tori to be happy like the old Tori I knew.

"Hey, I didn't want to keep you. I just wanted to call and let you know that my mom was okay."

"Really?"

"Yeah, it ended up being endometriosis. Instead she was able to keep everything so she didn't need a hysterectomy and she's fine, but I certainly would have taken that over cancer."

"Oh, man, that's good, girl."

"I know and I had to tell you that. I also wanted to tell you thanks for being so cool when I called. You were there for me, Perry, and you told me we were going be friends and I now understand what that means. When I needed you, you were right there to give me uplifting words that I wouldn't have gotten from the hospital. When you told me to rely on God, it really meant a lot, so friends?" she said.

And I truly felt she meant it at that moment. After all we'd been through, after all we messed up, separately and together, I was ready for us to be friends and it looked like she was, too. Believing her I responded, "Sure, friends."

"Well, alright, I'm going to let you go."

And just like that the conversation was over. I was not going to be late to this meeting with Coach and he didn't actually give me the gold jersey to wear. At that moment we were all wearing white, no blue, no gold, just white.

"You would have a fan spot booth set up by yourself. The media and the people wanted to meet you so we thought it best to give you your own line. You'll be able to handle all, that right?"

"Yes, sir."

"Well, let's get on over there and let our fans know we plan to win this season."

I nodded. I didn't know if I was supposed to ride up with him, ride in my own car, walk, or what, so I just sort of stood in his office and scratched my head.

"Oh, I need you to ride over with some special fans of yours, okay."

I wasn't so hip on all the NCAA rules but me riding with fans didn't seem right, but coach told me to do it. I mean, what did I know? But then I could've chuckled on my thoughts when I saw my own parents walk through his door. Yeah, they definitely were my biggest fans and I'm sure we'd be in compliance if I rode with them. I rushed up to my mom and gave her a big hug like the first time she picked me up from preschool or something.

"Coach Red, you treating my boy right? He's hugging his mother awful tight."

"Yeah, they tend to appreciate you guys after they're up here with me for a while, but as you can see, he's completely healthy and doing fine. I'll meet you guys over there in a second. Feel free to use my office; my secretary is right outside the office. She'll lock up."

"Thanks, Coach," I said to him.

Both of them started asking me questions back and forth. I couldn't even answer any of them, and I couldn't really hear what they were asking me. I just saw their mouths moving overtime. I was cool, I was fine, but I didn't know how my dad was. When he grabbed my mom around the waist and kissed her in front of me, I could see they were still honeymooning, and that was certainly a great sight to see, but what about business? People weren't going to bring it up when they needed to.

"I hear y'all, I see y'all, but for real, Dad, what's up?"

"What you mean, son?"

"Come on, Dad."

"Your dad is fine."

"Mom, you don't have to protect me."

"Oh yeah, we're going through the motions to sell the dealership, but I got some cool things in the works. I applied to be a janitor at your old school, Lucy Laney. Here I come," he teased.

"Oh see, you got jokes. Seriously, man, I'm alright. Let's get over here at this fan day and let them meet you."

"Oh yeah, I know you back in full swing. I heard you showed out yesterday."

"Dad, I'm straight. My question is, are you?"

"I couldn't lie to my second good bullet, right? When things getting a little bit more confirmed, I'll let you in on it. For now just know God's got it. That's enough for you, right?"

"Yes, sir."

"Patricia, do you know this son of yours is now a man?"

"I'm looking at him, he looks taller and wider, and of course, my baby is handsome."

"Oh well, you could of left that part out."

"Dad," I said.

"Naw, son, I really respect the fact that you were there for me. God sent me an angel that night," he told me as my mom walked ahead of us, "and that angel ended up being my son. Keep up with Him and you can go far, right?"

Again I nodded.

Coach told me I would have my own little setup on fan day but for real it felt like I was a star or something. I had a booth, Deuce had his own space, Mario had a corner and tow of our defensive players. The rest of the team was nestled under a big tent together. They all had their own seat but it wasn't primetime and I wished I was over there to blend in. Coach asked me if I could handle it. Maybe I should have said no, but every person that came up to me was saying how they couldn't wait to see me play. They knew I'd do great for the school and for one man in particular. He had sandy red hair and his little boy was with him.

"The first time y'all scrimmaged, my wife came and brought our son. He came back with stories about how the players were using all kinds of bad language that wasn't stuff we allowed him to say."

Then I remembered the little kid.

"I had heard about you and told him to look out for Perry Skky Jr., our new rookie, and he told me you were on the sidelines near him and that you came over and shook his hand, and when some of the players were using bad language, you looked just as mad as he did. I guess I'm trying to say you got character. I knew it wasn't easy for you coming back off your injury that's been plaguing you for a while. We've been praying for you, son, and we'll continue to do that throughout the course of this season. This school needs more players like you."

I nodded once again but that time in humility.

Wow, God had brought me here for more than to just play football, I had a responsibility to be a role model and He sent that man and his son over here to tell me I was doing okay.

Finally fan day was over. We were out there for three hours. It was supposed to only be two, but the overwhelming crowd made us want to stay and greet everyone. As soon as I walked away from the table, I saw Lance. He looked me straight in the eye and I thought he was just going to walk the other way. I mean, it was just his MO. He and I were getting along better, but we still weren't best friends or anything. However, he actually walked over to me. I didn't know what he was going to say but I was bracing myself for it not to be nice. He extended his hand.

"So, I owe you congratulations, huh?"

"Naw, man, you don't have to do that."

"Yeah, I do. You beat me out of two categories."

"You'll be starting soon. You should be starting now. We all know you were laps around Mario at training camp."

"I know you think so. I saw you cheering me on and the pep talks you gave me when I was down. Man, for real, there is no way I can be mad at you that you're going to start. 'Cause I can't wait to now be out there starting with you throwing you the ball. Yesterday you were so bad when you did that one move,"—and Lance displayed it—"that was lateral."

My whole body extended and grabbed the ball that was too wide.

"I was like dang he's tight!"

"You said I beat you out in two ways. What do you mean?"

"Well, you're on first string before me. Which is going to help me because it's going to push me to get there myself." Both of us could only chuckle at that.

"Well, what was the other thing?"

"Well, my line wasn't long enough. I got to talk to a beautiful girl."

"I'm not following you."

"Savoy is here, okay! You and I know she's crazy about you and I know you crazy about her the way you threw away our friendship right in the beginning when you knew I had interest in her, too."

"I'm sorry about that, man."

"You can't help what your heart feels, and I'd be crazy to stand in the way of what y'all need to build. She's a cool girl. I mean, I ain't ready to settle down or anything like that anyway and at first I thought that was the plan she was on, but she was looking for you."

"She ain't come over in my line, I searched the line. That's her style."

"That's probably why I like her, too."

"So, you and me straight?"

"Yeah, we straight. Anytime you get on my nerves, I'm just going to come in your room and hit you across the head with a pillow or eat all your food."

"Boy, you silly. I would've bought that, too."

"I got a little cash, we ain't broke and all. My dad would ring my neck if he knew I was misusing the funds he scraped up to give me for that. I got the house next month."

"Boy, you crazy," I said to him.

"I know what's right, I know what I'm supposed to do, but sometimes I just lose my way, but shoot, Perry, you helped me see the road I need to be on. You know the road that's pleasing to God, and you know, I like that. But do me a favor?"

"What's that?"

"Don't make Mario look too good out there or I won't never get to play. He throws them too high, too low balls—something got to drop. So I can get out there on that field and show 'em how it's done."

"Boy, you are silly. I hear you."

We slapped hands. When I found my folks, they were standing over by the Lees. Saxon was around, too, but I didn't see Savoy. Had she gone without speaking? Then I saw Saxon walking toward me. Lance and I were cool. After all, we weren't even competing for the same position, but Saxon and I were both wide receivers and I knew he desperately wanted to start.

"So, you the man now."

"Sax, I didn't know Coach was going—"

"You don't have to give me any excuses, boy. You deserve it."

"Yeah, but you been out there busting your butt day after day."

"Yeah, and I've never looked like you did yesterday."

"I think I'm better than Lenard but that's my battle."

"Seeing you in action like that, I'm not better than you."

"Whatever, man," I said to him, not even believing that I was hearing him say something positive.

"I mean, don't let it go to your head and all, but truth is the light." Once we took care of that, Saxon and I never had the kind of relationship that was easy for us to just keep talking. He sort of looked away. I started looking around. I didn't know what he was looking for, but I was definitely trying to find his sister.

"So, you do like Savoy, huh?"

"What, what do you mean?"

"I know you not looking for your parents. They right there, over there talking to mine. I know I put obstacles in y'all way. You hurt my sister, I know I did, I know, but I think you learned your lesson from that. She's coming up to school and there are a whole lot of chumps more like me than they are like you, and I guess I feel you are the lesser of two evils."

"So what are you saying?"

"I'm saying she went to the bathroom and you should go over there and wait for her, and when she comes out, surprise her. Handle your business. You hurt her again, though, I'll kill ya, and I won't have to worry about beating Lenard out for a spot because you won't be here to show up. You know what I'm saying?" As he poked his hand in my chest, I grabbed his hand and we held for a second or two and it wasn't creepy. It was one of mutual respect. A couple of girls called Saxon's name and he said, "I'm gone. Take care of her."

"I got you."

"Yeah, I know."

I headed over to the girl's restroom and I waited for Savoy to come out although there were other females that came out before her and I could've choked when I saw Anna come up to me.

"Hey, Perry, I hadn't seen you in a while. I know you were doing your camp thing but I came here today to tell you to have a good season. Have you thought any more about what I said? I hadn't heard from you. You weren't waiting for me to come out of the bathroom, were you?"

And then Savoy came out. It was kind of awkward. She looked at me talking to the blond chic, and she was about to stroll right by, but I grabbed her arm.

"Naw, Anna, I wasn't waiting for you." I licked my lips. Holding my attraction to her. "I was standing out here waiting on this little lady right here. Anna, this is Savoy, the girl who's got my heart."

"Wow," Anna said, taken back. "Well, I can certainly see why. She's beautiful."

"Do you go to Tech?"

"Well, I will be, so yeah."

"Oh wow, me too. Maybe I'll see you in class sometime," Anna said, being very nice. "I'll see you later, Perry." Anna waved to Savoy, and Savoy waved back.

"The girl who has your heart?" she said to me, smiling.

"I didn't want to overstep and say more. You said you'd be back in a few weeks and it has taken forever."

We walked around the corner to a private place and I just planted my lips on hers. When the kiss was finished, we kissed again. As my tongue slid down her throat, it felt like that was the only place it was supposed to be and it didn't want to leave home, but it had to.

"So where do we go from here?" I asked her. "From that kiss, I can tell you want to give me another chance."

"You can, huh?" she teased back. "Like football, let's just play it by ear."

"When I play football, I play to win."

"Well, as good of a player you are, you know I'm on your team, right?"

"Seriously, Savoy you know I'm sorry, right? About every-thing."

"I know."

We went to meet up with our parents and it was hard to talk to them because different fans leaving the field kept giving me accolades. My mom and Savoy were checking me out to make sure it wasn't going to my head and it wasn't. I had come from such a long way, the bottom really. It just felt good getting some encouragement.

~ 15 ~
Doing Life Right

Savoy and I had a great night together hanging out with our families and laughing as we went through the grocery store for food for her room. I just couldn't believe that this time she was here to stay, since the other times she'd been down here, she'd always had to go back to Aiken. She and her brother were going to share a car, and since he had it, I had the honor of taking her back to her place.

"I got to help you take up the groceries," I said to her, not wanting our time together to end.

"You know, I need to ask you something." Her friendly demeanor suddenly went serious.

I could honestly say I had to take a deep breath. What was going on with her now? Sometimes females tripped me out. They overanalyzed things, couldn't leave well enough alone, and though I didn't want to make trouble where there was none, I knew something was up so I looked away.

"You have a problem with me wanting to talk to you?"

"No, I don't. I just liked where we were, you know."

"And I want us to stay at that place," she said. "I want us to be able to talk about our problems."

"So now you're concerned?"

"Perry, don't get upset."

"Alright, what you want to know?"

"The girl you were talking to earlier."

I looked dumbfounded.

"Oh, don't act like you don't know what I'm talking about. When we were at fan day and I came out of the bathroom, you were talking to this girl. She really looked like she knew you. How did she? Tell me the story."

"Oh, this is where this is going."

She wanted to know about Anna. She didn't seem jealous at the time, but I should have realized the whole too-nice-at-first introduction would be revisited. How was I going to tell her how I knew Anna? I mean, it was that girl's personal business that I didn't want to just put out there, and though I trusted Savoy, it wasn't my business to tell.

"You're not talking. Did you guys date some? You met her when you first got here, I mean, what?"

"She was just a girl I had an encounter with. It's no big deal, nothing to worry about. Again I even told her in front of you how much you mean to me. There's no need to talk about this."

"Yeah, we do. I want to get us on the right track, and if that's your aim, that's your mission, then you need to talk to me. I don't want any other surprises with a girl like I did back home."

"Well, you had been going out with Lance. I haven't even asked if that is completely over?"

"So, because I went out with a white, you decided to go out with a white girl, is that it?"

"No, you want to know the story, here it is. When I went down to Hilton Head for the summer, you remember that's when we went to the movies and you was tripping, acting crazy."

"Oh, so you went on vacation and talked to the first girl you see?"

"No, I was running and jogging on the beach and I came across some girl that looked all upset and hurt or something, I went over to her, and sure enough, she was raped. I just tried to help her out and that's how I know her. It turns out that she goes here."

I couldn't bring myself to tell Savoy the rest of the story about me getting assaulted by white guys because they thought I was the one that assaulted Anna. She asked me how I met the girl and I was upfront and honest about how we came to connect. The next thing I know, I got a big embrace by my girl.

"I'm sorry, I just wanted to know."

"It's cool, I know I still got to earn your trust."

She kissed me on the cheek and said, "I trust you."

On the way back to my place my cell rang, "What's up, sis?" I said when I saw the number.

"I hear my brother is going to be the starting wide for the Yellow Jackets. You go, boy."

"You heard that, huh?"

"Yeah, Dad is so proud of you."

"What's up with my boy?"

"He's cool and y'all cool?"

"Yeah, yeah. We cool."

"We're good."

"A'ight, a'ight. Just making sure my big sis is taken care of."

"You know I can handle my own. What kind of trouble are you getting into down there?"

"I'm straight."

"How about with Savoy? She's at Tech now right?"

"Actually I just dropped her off."

"For real?"

"Yeah."

"We might have another chance."

"Well, don't blow it this time."

"Yeah, you right. So what's up?"

"Naw, I just wanted to let you know that I was proud of you. I want you to win every single game you play in except the game when y'all play against us, of course."

"Oh, so when we play the Bulldogs, you not gonna cheer for your brother?"

"No!"

"Oh, that's cold."

"You know I will, but umm, how do you feel about Dad and the dealership?"

I had forgot that I hadn't talked to my sister about the whole thing.

"At least we get to keep our cars," I told her.

"Dad seems so positive about it. I talked to him one time and he seemed like it was the end of the world for him. But now it's like good riddance; he's excited to have new opportunities."

"What, what new opportunities? He hadn't told me anything."

"Well, he hasn't really told me anything either, but Mom says he's got something cooking and it looks pretty good. I don't know. We should just keep praying for him. He's too young to retire, plus you know I need money for clothes."

"Yeah, me too," I joked.

When I pulled up to my place, I was still talking to Payton, but I couldn't believe my eyes. It was Cole and Damarius.

I said to her, "Well, you take care, girl. I got to go. My boys are here."

"Awh see, you and the football team are already getting close."

"Naw, I got visitors from home. Damarius and Cole are up here."

"What, don't get into any trouble with them two there."

"Bye, girl."

"A'ight, love you, babe."

"Love you too, girl."

"What's up?" I said as I got out of my car to greet my two friends. "Y'all ain't call a brother to let me know y'all was gonna be in town."

"We tried to make it to your fanfare day."

"Fan day," I said to Damarius.

"Well, whatever. We just had to come when Cole got some time away from the Gamecocks. He swooped through, picked me up, and we're here. We met some of your teammates, though. We asked how your leg was doing and all that good stuff."

"You can't call your boys when you get good news," Cole said to me. It hurt for me to see his leg in a cast.

"And how did you drive all banged up?"

"Well, it's my right one. I can still do everything with my left one. Then when I got to Augusta, Damarius drove us here, but you a starter, man, that's so good."

"Cole," I said as I went over to put my hand on his shoulder. "It'll be you in a minute."

"Well, we came to give you some news of our own."

"It's not my ACL, it's just my PCL that's torn."

"*What?*"

"Yeah, I might get back in at the end of the season. You just kept me positive and thinking of the best."

"I was talking all negative before I even got the results back."

"You chump," I said as I hit him in the stomach.

"Coach gave us a few days off before the classes start so I wanted to come up and let you know."

"What you into these days?" I looked at Damarius and asked.

"Well, you know I had to retake the graduation exam and take some summer school, and umm, I didn't pass."

Gosh, that hurt me to hear. I couldn't believe that I heard it. Then Cole started smiling and Damarius started laughing.

"What the heck is so funny?"

"He's lying to you, man."

"Boy!"

"I passed!"

"Oh man, give me some." Then we did our usual dap and embrace.

We went over to Atlantic Station and ate at the Sports Bar and Grill; no alcohol, no girlies, just clean home boy fun.

"So you know he had his trial, too," Cole said as we were sitting around eating hamburgers and hot wings.

"Naw, it seems like I missed everything trying to get myself together. How'd it go?"

"Man, I just had to tell the truth. Jayboe is going to be away for a while and now I have to get out of town before he gets one of his boys to retaliate on me."

"Dang, man" I thought, "So what you gonna do?"

"I got an old high school coach to give me a chance at Fort Valley."

"So you gonna get to go?"

"Yeah, he wants me to be there next week. He says I got Division One talent in me and that he could really use me to help his team, so we'll see."

"Boy, that's awesome."

"Hopefully we'll have a biweek and we can check out each other's games. Being that I missed all of training camp, I might not play."

"I'm sure you'll find a way out there on the field," Cole said to him.

"Yeah, you will."

Three boys from Augusta, Georgia: three backgrounds, three different abilities, and three different dreams, but we were all on the same track. The one that would lead us somewhere positive. It was a good thing.

* * *

Time was flying. I couldn't believe my summer was almost over, my parents were just up here for fan day, and now it was the day of the last scrimmage. Practice had been going well, Savoy and I had talked just enough, I got the class schedule I wanted. Life was grand. But when my dad told me he was on his way up here to tell me something pretty important, I just prayed. His voice didn't indicate either way whether it was a good or bad thing, but he had gone through so much I didn't need to think that for sure this was going to be good news. Deep down I knew I couldn't give up on God. I knew I had to keep my father encouraged, whether the news was encouraging or not. I was learning that being a believer truly was a faith walk, and as I learned this past summer, the mind is ready to handle all that life brings. You need to stay connected to the body of Christ. We all need a positive word sometimes. Every day in our life isn't going to be a grand one, but we must seek the best in people, don't look down on folks, and know that you are no better than the next man. And if we understand that God blesses us all in different ways, the ups and downs in life can be a little more tolerable.

I went to my dad's hotel for breakfast. "Mom didn't make the trip?" I said to him.

"No, she's doing something with her sorority. She knew you'd do well."

"So Dad, I can't hold in the suspense any longer. What's going on? You all right?"

"Son, I got great news. Mercedes-Benz is trying to get more African-American dealers. Somehow they got my name, knew that I was selling my dealership, and I was having issues corporately. They found out my beefs and brought me to the headquarters here. We talked a little and they want to add a dealer right outside Augusta. The financing plan is in place and the money I get from selling the dealership will be enough to put into it. They gonna match some of my capital.

You don't have to wait until you're an NFL player, boy, to buy a Mercedes."

"Dad, that's awesome," I said as I took my hand and hit his. "I'm so excited for you."

"I know you are, son. I know I scared you a lot a few weeks back. I still been thinking about that night and I cringe at the fact that you saw me at my lowest moment."

"Aw, Dad, don't worry about that."

"Well, that's the thing, son, a man's pride is heavy at times. But I've been praying and praying for you to become a man in my eyes; not that I thought you were a prankster, not that I thought you took life not seriously at all, but something along those lines. And I had no idea God was going to answer my prayer in a way and manner in which He did, seeing you step up, show up, and give encouragement like that. Well, let's just say I know you're ready to handle whatever comes your way."

"I don't know, Dad. I mean, I don't want to let you down either. I got the starting job, we got to scrimmage today, I just, I don't know. Because of everything you went through, I've been paranoid of white people up here at Tech. I just, I don't know, everywhere I would go, everybody would put me in this group and in that group and sometimes I was isolating myself and I'm trying to get past all that and through all that. I just don't want to make bad choices. I don't want to let you down, I don't want to let Coach Red down. I don't want to let God down."

"Being a man ain't easy. I was rushing it and I don't know why. I understand," he said, surprising me. No lecture about me and my pity party, just truth. He understood—men didn't have to be strong all the time. "You saw that life isn't fair and that every Christian doesn't do right all the time. People are going to treat you differently because you're starting. People might treat you differently when they find out we gonna step it up with the dealership, leave the no-name cars and get the brand name. Which, you know, as long as the thing has four wheels and rides, who cares? Some people do and we hope to make more dollars on those, but some people treat you different because of your skin color, people would even treat you differently because of your gender. I mean a black man has it hard. That is just the way it is, but son, the character of a man's heart far outweighs his wallet, his skin color, or his status on the football team. I'm a little glad that you're humbled."

"What do you mean?"

"Well, when you were hurt, you had to sit on the sideline, and now you know how that feels, and when one of your teammates has to go through that, you'll be able to tell him it'll be alright. We had a scare thinking we were going to the poor house, maybe be homeless or something."

"Dad, you silly," I said.

"Well, you know, I'm just keeping it real with you. You on a budget, you didn't go over on your limit. I don't even think you got hardly anything that shows you're growing up, son. If you can manage not having anything, you can manage having something, and I know it hurt you a lot when those guys attacked you out there on the beach. I hadn't brought it up. I've been going through stuff. You know that. You didn't press charges. You just prayed and let God deal with it, and sometimes that's what we have to do—walk away from things. We can't fix every situation, but we can certainly try and do our part to make the world a better place."

We went on to eat our breakfast and talked about the upcoming schedule and about how Mom felt about the dealership, and of course, he told me she couldn't wait to ride in style. He even told me he was going up to see Payton later on after my game. I couldn't believe I knew before my sister. As tight as the two of them were, it was good for me to make strides with my father. As I was growing a relationship with my Heavenly Father, I was getting blessed two times over because I was getting a chance to grow with my Earthly Dad as well, and boy, did that mean a lot to me.

He said some things over breakfast that meant a lot to me, most importantly if I took care of me and did the best I could, God would handle the rest. And as God showed up for my family by giving my dad another chance with a greater deal, seeing God this time clearly let me see I'm through every time and sometimes He made us go through the tough stuff to make us better.

"I am proud of you, son," my dad said before I left the hotel to head back to campus. "Very proud."

I held back my tears, thankful that he hadn't taken his life that other night. Yeah, I was growing, maturing, trying to be somebody's man, but I still was a guy who needed his pops. In that moment I knew my dad was going to be there.

"A'ight, boy, now get on out of here. I'll see you in a bit." We didn't hug.

I'm sure both of us knew we wouldn't be able to hold it together if we did, but that was okay. The gesture we didn't make confirmed the gesture we wanted to, and that was good enough for me. I could see in his eyes that he cared. Where the two of us were at, all was right within the world.

As I stood in the locker room getting dressed along with the team, I had my earplugs in listening to my iPod to music that would keep me encouraged. As I put on my cleats, I thought, "Lord, thank you for giving me another chance to get out there and play the game I love. Looking around this locker room, I have come to care about a lot of these guys. You know how important these scrimmages are to us. Keep us safe. Make us all shine. Sometimes it feels like I ask for the impossible, but I know with you, all things are possible."

I had finished my prayer but didn't get to finish it in the

right way because I was tapped on my shoulder. I turned around and saw Lenard standing over me. I stood up and let my 6-foot-four-inch frame tower over his 6-foot-1. The competitive spirit just sort of kicked in the way he was eyeing me, as if he couldn't wait to get out there on the field and make Coach Red look like he'd made the dumbest decision in his life upgrading me to first team. But then something inside me, probably the Holy Spirit, calmed down the fighting spirit that was about to go off on Lenard. I had just prayed for everybody, everybody including the other wide receiver, and though I knew Lenard wasn't really, really trying to be down to walk with God, I knew I was.

"So I know you can't wait to get out there and try to show me up?" Lenard smirked and rolled his eyes at me. "But I got my A game on today for you freshmen. I know your little friend Saxon is trying for my spot, but the way I plan to play today, he'll probably take yours before he'll take mine. Actually there's no probably in it. You gonna look crazy trying to keep up with me!"

"You know what though, Lenard? I want you to do well."

"What?" he said, stepping back a few feet.

"Yeah, last scrimmage I remember defense made offense look, like you said, crazy, stupid, and unable to perform. You show out and offense looks good. We're on the same side of the ball. Do your thing."

Lenard started playing with his nose and then he licked his teeth. He looked me up and down. I guess he was trying to see if I was real or not, so I helped him out.

"I'm serious," I said as I placed a hand on his shoulder pad.

He was still pondering on what I had said and that was fine. He and I hadn't exactly been foes. I grabbed my helmet and left him to his thoughts, and as I dashed out on the field, I smiled. I didn't say what Perry wanted to say to Lenard. I did what God would do, and boy, didn't that feel good. Lance and Saxon were on special teams. I knew neither one of them wanted to play it. They also had to come against second-string defense, and at that point as the kick-off coverage team came blitzing at them, it was like our return team just froze. When offense went out on the field, we had to take the ball on the six yard line. Mario told me in the huddle that the ball was coming my way. First play he threw it to me twenty yards out. I met a DB and went in to score a touchdown. The largest crowd I had seen at our scrimmage went crazy. I knew my dad was up there somewhere very, very excited. I went over to the sideline and coach grabbed my helmet.

"That's why I got you here. Way to go."

The second-string offensive team of which Lance and Saxon were a part had no success. They were three and out and the next time we got the ball for our first-string offense, we were on our twenty yard line. Mario handed the ball off to Deuce and he ran it to the fifty. Next play from practice Mario threw a lateral to Lenard and immediately he was tackled. It was second and ten and Mario threw it to Lenard again and the pass was dropped. When we went back into the huddle, I got the call. Lenard looked over at me. I actually wished he'd get another chance, but when Mario took the snap and threw it to me in the corner of the end zone, I caught it for a second touchdown. And like déjà vu, the crowd went wild again.

As we jogged to the sideline, I happened to be running next to Lenard. I was surprised when he said, "Way to go."

I didn't even get a chance to tell him, "Hey, man, you'll get yours. You'll catch them passes like you had said and it'll be a great scrimmage day," because he jogged off faster, but it was something about how he said "way to go" that impressed me. Had he also gotten the concept that we were a team? Before Lance and Saxon went in, I went over to them and put my head right in between them both and said, "Warm-up time is over. Get out there and show 'em what you got."

Saxon turned around and gave me five and headed out onto the field with more stride in his step. Lance looked at me and said, "I don't know, Perry. I'm just nervous to run that ball. Some of those DBs are talking smack. I don't know, I don't know."

"Yeah, you do. You know you got what it takes inside of you to not let what they got to say to you get to you at all. Handle your business. If Sax wants the ball, throw it up in the air. Your arm is made of steel. Believe that you know who gave you the power." I pointed up to the sky.

Six plays later Lance threw a touchdown pass to Saxon. Deuce stood beside me on the sideline and said, "You need to be a coach. I heard you motivating them."

"Y'all motivated me when I was down."

"All I can say," Deuce said, "is for the rest of the ACC to look out for real."

The scrimmage ended pretty much the way I'd prayed for, and offense and defense had had great moments. Training camp was over and I was asked to be on Radio 790, the Zone, a local AM station that officially covered local sports. It was these two live brothers that I listened to often on the "Two Live Snooze" that were over in the press area doing a live feed. The marketing director and George came over and asked if I'd do an interview after the game. I had gotten some time to talk to my dad and talk some smack to the other players, shower, and then head up to go talk to the two crazy guys: Rod and Dee.

"So, we've got Perry Skky Jr. here with us on the 'Two Live Snooze,' and we just want to let you know we keep it real," the older brother, Dee, said.

"But I must say, as a former Yellow Jacket myself," Rod cut in and bragged, "you were really holding it down. Majorly impressive, exceeding all of the expectations the coaching staff had for you. We just hoping you gonna stay with us for four years."

"Yeah, right," his brother Dee cut in and said. "You know he gonna leave in three and go get them big dollars."

"Have you thought about anything like that, Perry?"

"Well, just being a freshman, college life is a big change for me. I can't think of anything more than the first couple of games of the season that we play these first couple of weeks."

"This freshman class that you have here at Tech," Dee began, "is one of the best in years, and I know coming out of high school being a top recruit like you were, there were a lot of other athletes all hoping to increase their stock in fulfilling their dream and get to play on Division One level. Any words of wisdom you want to give to them?"

"Yeah, just keep a level head, keep a level ground on your books and your skills. For me I'm trying to stay prayed up."

"Uh-oh, Rod, we got a Christian in the house," Dee said. "I wish you would have told us. I would have gotten the heathen out of here."

"Ha ha ha!" Rod exclaimed. Obviously the two brothers were crazy, but very cool.

"Well, what about as a young black guy facing challenges—learned anything with that? I know you were at an all-black school and now you're here at Tech. Actually that's an interesting question."

I began, "I learned that segregation in any form is wrong. We all have good and bad things about us, but I think the object to this life is to be the best that you can be more than you are at your worst. And the only way for that to happen is to not worry about the color of someone's skin, and when I hang out with people because of their income brackets, I get it wrong. When I hang out with only starters, I get it wrong.

For me if I am with any clique, it's going to be with ones who believe in the Lord."

"Sounds like you truly got your head together, bruh," Dee said in a serious tone.

"I appreciate that man because it's tough trying to be a guy with character."

Dee asked, "Any last thing you want to say?"

I sighed and thought about my crazy summer and summed it up in one statement: "We all mess up sometimes, but if we make a conscious effort to do good more times than not, we'll be doing life right."

Perry Skky Jr., Book 3:

PROBLEM SOLVED

Stephanie Perry Moore

ABOUT THIS GUIDE

The following questions are intended to
enhance your group's reading of
PERRY SKKY JR.: PROBLEM SOLVED
by Stephanie Perry Moore

DISCUSSION QUESTIONS

1. Perry Skky Jr. finally sees that equality isn't given to everyone. Do you think he overreacts or doesn't react strong enough to the hotel manager wanting him to settle down? How do you stand up for what's right?

2. Perry speaks at his Baccalaureate service. Do you think he challenged his peers correctly? What would you say to your friends to get them to strive for greatness?

3. At a swim party, Perry gets upset when he catches his cousin and his friend getting busy. Do you think he handled the situation right? What are ways to protect those you love without being confrontational?

4. In Hilton Head, Perry sees a girl in trouble and tries to help, yet he is attacked for his kindness. Looking back, if he had the chance to help again, do you think he should? What limits would you go to in order to help a stranger?

5. Perry is angered at the racism he learns goes on in business. What were the issues the other minority dealers had? What are suggestions you have that could make sure everyone is treated equally regardless of color, economic status, gender, or religion, etc.?

6. Perry finds his dad at the end of his rope because he is losing his family business. Do you think Perry was wise in stepping in to help his dad while his dad had a gun? How has God used you to help others find the joy in their tough situations?

7. Perry is bombarded with media when he gets to college. How do you feel he handles the press? How can you stay grounded when life becomes surreal?

8. Perry hurts himself at summer practice. How does he find joy in his pain? Can you remember a time when God took your bad circumstance and made something wonderful?

9. The football is divided between the starters and the second and third-string players? Do you think Perry is responsible for lifting up his teammates and working out the drama? What does the bible say about peacemakers?

10. Perry and Savoy realize they want to make their relationship work. Do you think with Perry's status as a player they will be able to maintain their relationship? What are ways to have healthy dating relationships?

Start Your Own Book Club

Courtesy of the PERRY SKKY JR. series

ABOUT THIS GUIDE

The following is intended to help you get
the Book Club you've always wanted
up and running!
Enjoy!

Start Your Own Book Club

A Book Club is not only a great way to make friends, but it is also a fun and safe environment for you to express your views and opinions on everything from fashion to teen pregnancy. A Teen Book Club can also become a forum or venue to air grievances and plan remedies for problems.

The People

To start, all you need is yourself and at least one other person. There's no criteria for who this person or persons should be other than having a desire to read and a commitment to read and discuss during a certain time frame.

The Rules

People tend to disagree with each other, cut each other off when speaking, and take criticism personally. So, there should be some ground rules:

1. Do not attack people for their ideas or opinions.

2. When you disagree with a book club member on a point, disagree respectfully. This means that you do not denigrate another person for their ideas. There shouldn't be any name calling or saying, "That's stupid!" Instead, say, "I can respect your position, however, I feel differently."

3. Back up your opinions with concrete evidence, either from the book in question or life in general.

4. Allow every one a turn to comment.

5. Do not cut a member off when the person is speaking. Respectfully wait your turn.

6. Critique only the idea (and do so responsibly; again, simply saying, "That's stupid!" is not allowed). Do not criticize the person.

7. Every member must agree to and abide by the ground rules.

Feel free to add any other ground rules you think might be necessary.

The Meeting Place

Once you've decided on members, and agreed to the ground rules, you should decide on a place to meet. This could be the local library, the school library, your favorite restaurant, a bookstore, or a member's home. Remember, though, if you decide to hold your sessions at a member's home, the location should rotate to another member's home for the next session. It's also polite for guests to bring treats when attending a Book Club meeting at a member's home. If you choose to hold your meetings in a public place, always remember to ask the permission of the librarian or store manager. If you decide to hold your meetings in a local bookstore, ask the manager to post a flyer in the window announcing the Book Club to attract more members if you so desire.

Timing is Everything

Teenagers of today are all much busier than teenagers of the past. You're probably thinking, "Between chorus rehearsals, the Drama Club, and oh yeah, my job, when will I ever have time to read another book that doesn't feature Romeo and Juliet!" Well, there's always time, if it's time well-planned and time planned ahead. You and your Book Club can decide to meet as often or as little as is appropriate for your bustling schedules. *Once a month* is a favorite option. *Sleepover Book Club* meetings—if you're open to excluding one gender—is also a favorite option. And in this day of high-tech, savvy teens, *Internet Discussion Groups* are also an appealing option. Just choose what's right for you!

Well, you've got the people, the ground rules, the place, and the time. All you need now is a book!

The Book

Choosing a book is the most fun. PROBLEM SOLVED is of course an excellent choice, and since it's part of a series, you won't soon run out of books to read and discuss. Your Book Club can also have comparative discussions as you compare the first book, PRIME CHOICE, to the second, PRESSING HARD, and so on.

But depending upon your reading appetite, you may want to veer outside of the Perry Skky Jr. series. That's okay. There are plenty of options, many of which you will be able to find under the Dafina Books for Young Readers Program in the coming months.

But don't be afraid to mix it up. Nonfiction is just as good as fiction and a fun way to learn about from where we came without just using a history text book. Science fiction and fantasy can be fun, too!

And always research the author. You might find the author has a website where you can post your Book Club's questions or comments. You can correspond with Stephanie Perry Moore by visiting her website, www.stephanieperrymoore.com. She can sit in on your meetings, either in person, or on the phone, and this can be a fun way to discuss the book as well!

The Discussion

Every good Book Club discussion starts with questions. PROBLEM SOLVED, as will every book in the Perry Skky Jr. series, comes along with a Reading Group Guide for your convenience, though of course, it's fine to make up your own. Here are some sample questions to get started:

1. What's this book all about anyway?

2. Who are the characters? Do we like them? Do they remind us of real people?

3. Was the story interesting? Were real issues of concern to you examined?

4. Were there details that didn't quite work for you or ring true?

5. Did the author create a believable environment—one that you could visualize?

6. Was the ending satisfying?

7. Would you read another book from this author?

Record Keeper

It's generally a good idea to have someone keep track of the books you read. Often libraries and schools will hold reading drives where you're rewarded for having read a certain number of books in a certain time period. Perhaps a pizza party awaits!

Get Your Teachers and Parents Involved

Teachers and parents love it when kids get together and read. So involve your teachers and parents. Your Book Club may read a particular book where it would help to have an adult's perspective as part of the discussion. Teachers may also be able to include what you're doing as a Book Club in the classroom curriculum. That way books you love to read such as PROBLEM SOLVED can find a place in your classroom alongside the books you don't love to read as much.

Resources

To find some new favorite writers, check out the following resources. Happy reading!

Young Adult Library Services Association
http://www.ala.org/ala/yalsa/yalsa.htm

Carnegie Library of Pittsburgh
Hip-Hop!
Teen Rap Titles
http://www.carnegielibrary.org/teens/read/booklists/teenrap.html

TeensPoint.org
What Teens Are Reading?
http://www.teenspoint.org/reading_matters/book_list.asp?sort=5&list=274

Teenreads.com
http://www.teenreads.com/

Sacramento Public Library
Fantasy Reading for Kids
http://www.saclibrary.org/teens/fantasy.html

Book Divas
http://www.bookdivas.com/

Meg Cabot Book Club
http://www.megcabotbookclub.com/